SHAMELESS

A REVERSE HAREM FANTASY ROMANCE

DEVYN SINCLAIR

Copyright © 2019 Devyn Sinclair

All rights reserved.

No part of this book may be reproduced in any form or by any electronic or mechanical means, including information storage and retrieval systems, without written permission from the author, except for the use of brief quotations in a book review. No part of this book may be used to create, feed, or refine artificial intelligence models, for any purpose, without written permission from the author.

CHAPTER ONE

KARI

I'm currently trying not to move, breathe, or give any indication that I am awake.

Lying on my side, I'm pressed between two men—men who somehow manage to achieve the impossible combination of sleeping deeply and lightly at once. For all the world, it always seems like they're passed out, but the second I give any sign that I'm awake, they're awake.

Constantly on the lookout for danger, even in sleep.

Thankfully, I feel a little better about that now. The magic that I've been learning to control wraps around us like a blanket, forming a shield that I can trust, even while unconscious. I'm hoping that gives my mates some peace of mind as well.

Two of my mates are currently sharing my bed. Urien is behind me, arm slung over my hip, and the warmth of his chest pressed against my back. Verys is in front of me, equally close. His silver hair has slipped down over his face, and I'm reminded of when I first saw him in my state of dizzy pain. I thought he was some sort of angel.

But I like the way they're holding me so near, solid heat and casual affection in their touch. And I don't want that to stop. These little moments of normalcy and intimacy are what I've come to crave the most. I love all of it—the fun and the sex and the way I'm slowly getting to know each of them for the men that they are. But at times like this—in the stillness—I can stop and realize that it's all real. This is my life now, and as crazy as that is, it's true.

Not that I imagine there will be much time for normalcy. Another reason I don't want to wake up. I'm pretending that everything outside of my bedroom simply does not exist. There's no one trying to kill me and steal my magic. There are no questions about what her bigger plan is. There's no worrying about the mate that no one else knows about. There's simply me, resting skin-to-skin with two of the men that I love.

And I do love them. I'm so in love them with them that if Odette and Emma actually knew they'd probably laugh and then pretend to vomit from the cuteness. I wouldn't even blame them for it.

The last few days have been great, especially the field trip I begged them to take to New York—only for an hour—to visit one of the sex toy stores there.

After Brae made the suggestion I couldn't get it out of my head, and it was well worth the amount of decoy portals that we had to create to get there. We haven't even had a chance to use some of the things they bought. Hell, I'm not even sure that I know all the things that they brought back with them.

Looking at Verys again, I can't help myself—I reach out very slowly and brush the hair out of his eyes. He opens them in response, just like I knew he would, but he closes them again, smiling softly. "Took you long enough."

"I didn't want to wake you."

"I was already awake."

I roll my eyes. "How?"

"Your breathing changes," he says softly.

"I was trying really hard to keep it steady," I sigh.

"It was a good attempt," Urien says, pressing his lips to the side of my neck. "But we can tell."

"One of these days I'm going to figure out how to get you guys to *sleep in* without being injured and unconscious."

Verys chuckles. "Sleep is overrated."

"No," I say. "It's not. Sleep is amazing. And just laying here with you keeping me warm is fucking brilliant." Moving my fingers again, I brush the little bit of hair I missed away from Verys's eyes.

Urien moves away from me, and I miss the

warmth. He pulls me onto my back so I'm still nestled against him, but now he's looking down at me. Golden eyes flecked with silver hover above mine, bright in contrast to his dark navy skin. "I think I could prove that sleep is overrated."

He doesn't wait for me to answer, instead lowering his lips to my skin. The kiss is slow and sensual. Not immediately leading anywhere, just slow and pure enjoyment. No matter the speed, heat pools inside me, gathering deep as magic like night-kissed wind brushes across my skin.

Urien is a deliberate lover, every brush of his lips dripping with intention. And the slowness with which he moves his mouth and his magic across my collarbone is maddening, and delicious.

Verys presses his own kiss to my temple, and he laughs at my moan. But I can't help it—I love the way they make me feel. Even if it's something as simple as a kiss. I lean into his mouth, now caught between the two. There's no telling where is will go from here.

Urien moves his head lower, pushing aside the fabric of my nightgown. He has a plan, but I know that he won't tell me what it is.

There's a feeling then, someone drifting fingers across my cheek and a pulse of deep blue magic across my skin. I open my eyes to nothing. "Wait," I gasp. Urien looks up from where he's tracing the line of my ribs with his mouth. I manage to find the words "Wait. I felt something."

Verys smirks. "I would hope so."

"No," I shake my head. "Not you. Kiaran's magic."

They both freeze for a second, and then they're moving. Off the bed and pulling on clothes in a matter of moments. "Where?" Urien asks.

I shake my head again. "It was just magic. He may not even be here."

Verys's expression is hard. "The wards around this place are incredibly specific about what kind of magic is allowed through. None of his magic should be allowed through. No magic of any kind should be able to except yours, and ours."

Guilt gnaws at my stomach. By 'ours,' he means my fae mates. I need to tell them the truth about Kiaran, and why the wards are working exactly as they should. Hostile magic that he possesses—the kind that's driven by Ariana—can never reach me here. But that touch, and the dreams, those aren't the same. Those are just fragments of my mate reaching for me, and I want so badly to reach back.

But I'm afraid that if I do that I'll open a door that I can't close, and Ariana will be able to come through. It's not just me at risk if that happens, it's all of us. Maybe more. The Goddess didn't give me magic to hold and to wield for nothing.

"What's going on?" Kent stands in the doorway to my bedroom, holding what looks like a giant breakfast burrito. He takes in Urien and Verys at the ready, and I see him come alert.

"Nothing," I say, springing off the bed and twisting away from Verys's outstretched hands. "But that looks good, and I could use one."

I'm already halfway down the stairs before I hear their voices behind me, both Verys and Urien no doubt sharing with Kent what I would not. I'm choosing in this moment to still live in that happy little bubble that I woke up in—warm and happy.

Sure enough, the magic of the house has produced a whole platter of breakfast burritos that smell amazing. Egg and sausage and cheese. It's a perfect blend of flavors, and I silently thank the magic for giving me what I didn't even know that I needed. It nearly always manages to do that, and it's amazing.

I'm curled up in my favorite spot on the couch, absolutely stuffing my face when they all come down the stairs together like my own private army. Brae looks like he's still half-asleep, but jumped up when the rest of them told him there was danger. He could have slept. Aeric is laced with weapons and the barest sheen of sweat, like he's been training. Automatically, he stands in the doorway that leads to the rest of the house, ever the soldier.

"I'm sure everything is fine," I say. "There haven't been any more attempts on the wards, right?"

"For now," Verys says. "Although I think we might treat this like one."

"It wasn't," I say probably too quickly.

Brae's eyebrows raise and he scrubs the exhaustion from his face. "How do you know?"

I take a bite of burrito in order to give myself a moment. "I don't know how to explain it...the magic just didn't feel malicious."

They exchange looks that I pretend to ignore.

"What reason would he have to *not* be malicious?" Kent wonders out loud.

This is the moment where I should tell them the truth about Kiaran, but I can't. Anxiety churns in my gut. I don't know what they'll do. I trust them with my life, but Kiaran has already endangered mine more than once—even if it wasn't his choice. That's not an easy thing for anybody to get over. Especially the men who have dedicated themselves to keeping me alive. They're still a little battered from our last encounter, the last of the bruises fading on the fae, and Kent's are still colorful reminders of that battle.

The way they're looking at me right now, it's like

I can feel them staring right through my soul and knowing that I'm keeping something from them. It might be good that all our bonds are not sealed yet. But I haven't even told that I want to yet, and I should.

Quickly, I finish the breakfast burrito, once again silently thanking the magic of the house for giving me a perfect meal. "There's something that I wanted to talk to you guys about. I've been ignoring it, same way I've been ignoring everything for the past few days."

I like watching them array themselves across the space for this. Brae sits across from me, leaning his elbows on his knees, utterly focused. Aeric maintains his protective position and Kent has a similar stance, arms crossed, eyes moving like he's expecting Kiaran to jump out at any moment. Urien is relaxed and at ease, sitting with arms draped across the sofa, and Verys quietly sits nearby, steady as a rock.

I take a deep breath, a different kind of nerves jumping in my stomach now. Pulling my knees up to my chest, I wrap my arms around them. "When I was in that house with Kiaran, he figured out that you guys were close enough to hear me, and he told me that it didn't matter. That you'd been taken care of. And I decided that I never wanted to feel like that again."

Brae tilts his head, studying me with genuine curiosity. "What do you mean?"

The emotion that I felt in that moment comes flooding back, and I fight it back, even though the world blurs with unshed tears. "I mean that I didn't know if you were safe or hurt or dead, and that it was the same in reverse. There was no way for you to know that things weren't going the way we had imagined." I take a breath and swallow. "But I realized, that if I had sealed my bonds with you, that it wouldn't have been like that."

Around me, the air in the room goes still. It's like that moment before lightning strikes when the world feels like it's holding its breath until unleashing its power. In the same way, the men in front of me now are holding their breath together. "So I told myself if I made it out, that I would choose you. All of you. Whenever the time is right for each of us, to do that."

There's a moment of silence before Urien breaks it. "Really?" His voice is a whisper full of hope.

I nod, tucking my face into my knees. "Yes."

Arms come around me, and a hand guides my head back up and suddenly I'm kissing Verys and laughing because he steps aside for Urien and then Brae, all of them touching me in some way. I can feel the joy radiating from their hands and eyes, and I'm dizzy with magic and rightness that sinks down to my bones.

Until I look past them and see Aeric. He hasn't moved, and is staring straight at me, face hard. The tension rolling off him is obvious, like he's keeping himself in check. I can't decipher his expression. Pain and anger and something close to devastation.

One by one the other men see where my gaze has landed and they look too. Brae makes a connection that I must not understand, because he stands away from me. "Aeric—"

That's all he gets out. Aeric spins on his heel and goes up the stairs. Something is wrong. Up until now, everything he's told me and shown me made me think that this is what he wanted. Brae steps forward like he's about to go after him. "No," I tell him. "I think this is between him and me."

Kent rubs my back, hugging me close before I leave the couch. "He'll be fine."

"I thought this is what he wanted?" I'm not asking anyone in particular.

Brae nods. "It is. But there's…more to it than that."

"Okay." This time I'm addressing all of them. "I love you."

"Good luck," Kent says.

CHAPTER TWO

KARI

Following Aeric, I climb the stairs. We haven't spent much time in his bedroom, but that's the first place I go now, and I find him pacing. Not a casual pacing—it's a fervent stalking back and forth, and what feels like barely contained emotion simmering beneath the surface. But whatever it is, it's not directed at me.

Softly, I close the door behind me. Aeric's room is a deep burgundy, furnished with dark woods and rich leather. On one wall is an impressive array of weapons, and a workbench where it looks like he's in the process of making more. But the central feature of the room is the bed. It dominates the space with stark lines and four posts and speaks of dark and delicious things that could happen.

"Aeric." I speak because he hasn't stopped moving, and has barely seemed to acknowledge me. My first instinct is to ask him what's wrong, but I stop my words before they come out. The words that he spoke to me the first time we were in the crystal court appear in my mind as if they were called out of memory. *This is not the way I would have chosen. But I want you like I've wanted no other woman. And I have finished ignoring fate.*

This isn't something he can talk about. Not like this. Magic wells up from that place inside me, and with sudden clarity I know that it's the Goddess that called the memory to me. Aeric acts first. That's who he is. He's a fighter and right now he has nothing to fight. I don't know what he needs. He has to be the one to show me.

As he spins back towards me, I step directly in front of him so he stops short. It's like he's seeing me for the first time, and he freezes. Those gorgeous green eyes are full of turmoil that I don't understand, but it doesn't frighten me. "Take what you need, Aeric."

I'm against the wall in a second, his lips crashing down on mine. It's been forever since we were alone, and I realize with a shock that it's been him. He's been reluctant to touch me with the others. He's been separate, only touching me alone and then letting me go to the others. How did I not see it happening?

The thin nightgown that I'm wearing shreds under his hands so he can explore me, fingers finding my clit with bold determination. Mint green and aromatic spices flow over me with his magic, doing what he does so well and teasing me from the inside out. My nipples are already hard and pleasure is flowing up and out and I'm half-way to coming already.

Aeric places an arm across my chest, pressing me into the wall. I can feel the incredible strength that he holds, and that this time he's letting himself go further than he has before. One finger dips inside me, and I shiver. "More," I breathe.

His gaze flicks to mine, eyes dark with lust and power. "You don't have permission to speak unless you're asking to come."

Shock rolls over me, followed by a wave of white-hot arousal. Fingers work my clit in deliberate strokes, playing my body like an instrument. He presses harder against my chest, completely immobilizing me while he circles my clit, magic licking inside in time with his hand.

I close my eyes, unable to fight the rising tide of my orgasm, and I'm already gasping. Aeric is very good at what he does, already setting me on the edge of climax. "Please?" It's the only word I can form right now.

"Yes." His voice more of a growl than anything right now, but the roughness of it grates against my skin, adding to every sensation and sending me spiraling into pleasure. The orgasm hits me like a wall—fierce and furious and breathless. It spins downward through me too quickly, leaving me gasping in Aeric's grasp.

But he doesn't stop, barely pausing to grab my shredded nightgown from the ground as he pulls me to the bed. The energy rolling off of Aeric is different than I've seen before, and I'm not upset about it. It's a facet of him that I didn't know existed. But I want to know every facet of all my mates. I don't ever want them to hold back with me.

Aeric pulls my hands in front of me and wraps my wrists in the remnants of fabric, binding them together before he sheds his own clothes. He's so incredibly beautiful, and I don't know that I've ever had the chance to properly and thoroughly explore him. Pale green skin with darker, swirling marks like tattoos flowing over his back, arms, and shoulders. Hair that's such a dark green it shimmers like the feathers of an exotic bird. And eyes like the vibrant forest, pinning me in place as he reaches out, spins me and pushes me onto the bed on my knees.

With my hands tied this feels so much more vulnerable than otherwise, and I shiver. Aeric's hands skim my hips with his fingers before climbing up behind me. He doesn't wait or ease into his thrusts, he takes me in one thrust—just like I told him too. I moan, sinking deeper into the bed, unable to balance properly.

Aeric's chest is hard against my back, entirely heat and power and dominance. I'm bathed in waves of magic every time he drives into me, my own magic swirling up to meet his. It feels like all the oxygen in the world is gone. Aeric is fucking me, swift and brutal and I can't catch my breath. I'm drowning in him.

Fingers tangle in my hair and Aeric pulls me up onto my knees, not losing the furious pace that he's set. He slips that same hand around my throat. It's not a threat, just a restraint, holding me flush to his body while he takes what he needs. I lean back into him, surrendering to the feeling of him in control. My pussy is so wet that I'm dripping, and I'm thoroughly enjoying the feeling of being impaled.

The magic flowing through me is glowing under my skin—throwing shadows on the walls and spiraling into my gut. It steals my breath. Aeric's mouth is on my skin, biting lightly into my shoulder while his free hand once again finds my clit. I'm overloaded with sensation and on the brink of tumbling into another climax, so I force the words out that I know he expects. "May I come?"

Aeric bites harder, soothing the sting with his tongue before he groans a single syllable: "No."

My mind goes blank. I can't think, can't breathe, only try not to give in to what my body is begging to do. I reach for his hand—still stroking my swollen clit—to slow him down but my hands are bound and I am at his mercy. "Please, Aeric," I beg him. I can't take much more. Soon I won't have the choice.

Lips on my neck, rumbling on my skin. "You will wait for me."

I can't stay quiet anymore, my voice pouring out of me in moans and whispers, asking over and over again to come even though I know that the answer will be the same. He will tell me when he's ready. I'll ask anyway.

Aeric thrusts harder into me, and deeper, if that's even possible. He fills me completely, groaning with every move of his hips. "Now," he grits out. "Come with me now."

His magic flares in me and on me, carrying me over the edge and I collapse into bliss, unable to even scream. It's an eclipse of pleasure—it blocks everything else out. Aeric hollers his own climax, voice echoing off the walls and filling me with heat.

The fingers on my clit don't stop moving and so it feels like my orgasm doesn't stop. I'm shuddering and shaking and completely spent when Aeric slips out of me and lays down with me on the bed. He unties my hands and gathers me against his chest, both of us trying to catch our breath. That was visceral and needed. Almost feral.

My mate tilts my face up to his, kissing me with equal tenderness and heat. He rolls over me, pressing me down into the mattress with his weight, pinning me in place just as effectively as when he bound my hands. I raise an eyebrow. "That was different."

Aeric smirks, and it's the most normal that I've seen him today. "Bad different?"

No, that certainly wasn't bad. I bite my lip as I shake my head. "No. I just…I didn't know." He raises a questioning brow. "That you liked that kind of control. I mean I did, and I didn't." A blush rises to my cheeks and I stutter trying to get the words out. "You've held me in place before but never used… anything else."

He searches my face carefully before speaking. "You seemed to like that I did."

I don't think I've ever felt my face so hot. I never thought that I'd be the kind of girl to like that—being tied up—but then again, none of this is something that I thought I would be into. "Yes," I say. "Not every time, but yes."

He grins. "No, not every time."

Reaching up, I run my fingers through his hair. "If you like to be in control then why are you not—"

"In the Court of Dominance?" He finishes my question for me.

"Yeah."

I'm very distracted by his fingers, which are tracing patterns on my neck just below my ear. "Because my power still flows from physical pleasure, and not directly from the exchange of power. I like to be in control because I find it pleasurable, and I know what it can bring me…and you. But I don't desire submission the way someone in that Court would."

"Why do you like it?"

Aeric doesn't answer at first. He grabs my wrists in his hands and pulls them over my head, holding them there. In spite of myself my pulse kicks up a notch, and it's not lost on me that I can feel my heart beating between my legs. "Because of that," he says, leaning down and kissing my chest. "It sharpens pleasure. I like knowing that you're bound for me and no one else. That I have you exactly where I want you. That you're *mine*."

The word is so fierce that it makes my heart ache. I am his. But I'm not only his. Taking my hands back from him, he doesn't stop me when I raise his gaze to mine. "I need to know what happened," I say softly. "I thought you would be happy."

He looks away. "I am happy."

"It doesn't seem that way." He sighs, and I feel some tension comes back into his body. "Talk to me, Aeric. Please."

"I grew up in a family like this."

My eyebrows rise into my hairline. "Your mother had multiple mates?"

"No," he shakes his head. "Our situation is unique and rare, but she did have three different partners. And it—" A slow, even breath. "It was not easy. Even though her partners all loved her, they were not friends. Adding to the fire was the fact that she would not tell them who I belonged to. It caused resentment."

Now my heart is aching for a different reason. "Did they hurt you?"

"No. I wasn't as badly off as Verys, or others that I know. But there wasn't any investment or care either. Until my magic settled and proved whose child I was. But by then it was too little, too late.

"I swore that I would never do that. I would never be a part of a family like that. I wanted a *mate*. I wanted someone who was only mine. So there would never be any questions about loyalty or whose children were whose." He smiles at me gently. "And then there was you."

The moment hangs between us. It lasts forever and no time at all.

Slowly, softly, he brushes my mouth with his. "I didn't want to believe it. I couldn't fathom that it had happened. Not only that the Goddess had given me what I had asked for, but she'd done it in the way I'd wanted the least. I tried not to want you." He can't meet my eyes when he says that last part. "But there was never a moment I didn't. I knew from the moment I saw you, you were all there was for me."

He rests his head on my chest, and I hold him there, wrapping myself around him as best I can, blinking away tears. "Aeric, you know that I would never force you—"

"*No.*" The word comes from him fast as a whip. The raw look on his face matches his voice. "Don't say that. Don't ever doubt that I want you. That I *love* you. It's just that this isn't as easy for me as it seems to be for everyone else."

I laugh softly, snuggling down underneath him more so that our faces are closer. Without moving too much, Aeric reaches and pulls up a blanket over us together. "It's not easy," I say. "It's not. There's a reason we've been taking it slower. For me? Learning about all of you is a big job, and it's going to take time. I should have noticed it before."

Aeric kisses the sensitive space below my ear. "This isn't your fault. It's my history. And I'm lucky.

I'm sharing a mate with my closest friends. And I like Kent and Urien too. I just—" His jaw works, and he looks anywhere but at me. "I want you to be mine."

"I am yours," I tell him. When he looks at me I silence what he's about to say before he can even speak it. "I know that's not what you meant. But it's true. I am *yours*. I belong to you. But I belong to them too," I say softly.

"I know," he says. "I'm sorry."

I take his face in my hands and make sure that he's looking at me. "Jealousy isn't a crime. And it's not exactly avoidable in situations like this. We're all new at this, and figuring out what we need."

We rest together for a moment, and I can sense his relief, and his frustration. Despite his desire for me and for peace about my other mates, he can't help but feel how he feels. Magic is spinning in my gut, but it's not the Goddess's borrowed magic, it's mine. It's reaching for Aeric like a flower seeking the sun. Yearning for him. "I love you," I say. "So much that I don't understand it."

He looks at me, but says nothing. His arms curl underneath me, holding me closer.

"I can't promise to be only yours," I say.

For a moment Aeric looks stricken. "I would never ask you to do that."

"I know," I say, smiling. "But I can be only yours for a little while."

Aeric goes completely still in the way that only fae can do. "Kari."

"Bond with me." The words are out there, and I can't take them back. I don't want to. My little piece of magic leaps in response to the idea, stretching and purring, reaching out to Aeric's power almost without me helping it.

He's silent and still so long that I wonder for a moment if he's turned to stone. "If you want to," I finally add.

"Want to?" his mouth collides with mine, his magic blazing so bright I have to close my eyes against it. He's hard and aching between us, molding our bodies together so tightly I'm not sure where either of us end. "*Want* doesn't even begin to describe how I feel about that."

"And you'll be all right?" I ask. "When it happens with the others?"

"Right away? Probably not," he says, and I love him for being truthful. "But I will be, eventually. I'm not going to let history repeat itself. I love you too much, and respect them too much, for that."

"We'll cross that bridge when we get there. Right now it's just you and me," I say, and Aeric's self-satisfied smile makes me laugh. "You guys said it was—"

He takes the words out of my mouth. "A selfless act of pleasure. If you were fae, it would be mutual pleasure. But since you're human…" he trails off and places his lips to my ear with a whisper so soft it makes me shiver. "Do you have any idea how many times I've imagined your mouth on my cock?"

A tendril of his magic tangles with mine, small and intimate and sparking heat under my skin. I slip out from under his body and off the bed, reaching at the last moment to catch him by the hand and pull him with me. I'm moving on instinct, kneeling in front of him, those delicate coils of magic still linked together, twisting and dancing.

This feels important for him and me, this kneeling and this offering. And at the same time I know deep in my gut that this might not be the way it happens with the others. Sudden nerves sparkle along my spine. What will it feel like? To be bound to another person? Forever? Feel their emotions along with mine?

"Kari?" Aeric says.

I manage to laugh. "I don't think I've ever been nervous about a blow job before."

He strokes his hand through my hair. "I understand." Then he smiles. "But I'm still looking forward to it."

Aeric's cock is gorgeous up close, fading from a

dark green near the base to a much paler green near the head. He's thick too, and when I wrap my hand around him I marvel at the size. I haven't been this close to any of my fae mate's cocks except for Verys before he stopped me. The temptation is too big for me—I like being the source of that kind of pleasure.

Ignoring the nerves that are still jangling I lean forward and press my lips to his skin. Just the barest brush at first, breaking the contact barrier. Aeric hisses out a breath and the fingers still in my hair tighten. The tangled strands of our magic brighten, green and violet together, dancing.

Slowly, I drag my lips down Aeric's shaft and kiss my way back up. He's so hard that his cock jerks under my lips, and he groans. I smirk up at him. "I haven't even used my tongue yet."

I can see his jaw working as he grits his teeth. "I know."

The tail end of his words transform into a moan so raw it makes me wet just hearing it. I've covered him with my mouth, sucking just the tip. Aeric's fingers spasm in my hair before gripping. Tightening. Guiding me forward.

The nerves fade away as I sink down onto his cock. With Aeric guiding me, it all clicks into place. He likes to be in control, and with him, it seems, I like to give it. I like the sensation of his shaft gliding across my tongue and the friction of him slipping between my lips. Deeper, and deeper still.

I already taste him, traces of pleasure and magic that make their way onto my tongue. He tastes exactly what I imagine his power tastes like—like mint and Christmas spices and cardamom. I move faster, diving onto his cock and pulling back before taking all of him again, and Aeric lets me do it. His hand on my head—for the moment—is a reminder of his presence and his power and his control if he wishes to use it.

Aeric's gaze is locked on me. So when I look up at him—my mouth full of him—I'm treated to a look so full of lust that I start to shake. Energy is spinning back and forth between us at a pace I can't keep up with. The only thing I can do is focus on his cock, and I do.

I take him deeper, stretching myself to the limit to take as much as possible. I've always been good at this part. The few lovers I've had in the past have assured me of that, and Aeric's curse under his breath assures me of it now. His cock is at the back of my throat, and I can take more of him—can swallow him all the way, but I don't. It's instinct again, holding me back.

I need to taste him. Swallow his power by choice and not because I can deep throat him—though I will certainly be doing that in the future. I suck him harder, changing my rhythm to one that swings. Down fast, back slow, and again. I pause when I reach the head of his cock, brushing under it with my tongue, and I'm rewarded with seeing him shudder, abs in front of me tightening.

Magic pulses from me and from him, and I swear to the goddess that I can feel it beginning to merge and to bind. It's not scary the way I thought it might be. Instead it's soothing. I don't have any questions about what to do, only to keep going. Follow the mating instinct. That same impulse has me folding my hands behind my back and sucking him harder. Faster. Careening towards the inevitable end. A selfless act of pleasure.

I don't notice the moment that he takes control. It's so seamless that I can't doubt it. Aeric pulls my mouth deeper onto his cock while he thrusts his hips, and I relax into perfect peace and pleasure.

"Kari." My name is rough on his lips, and his movements become erratic. I look up at him to find his eyes locked on mine, and it's then that he comes. His hand fists in my hair and he holds his cock deep in my mouth, spilling heat and magic across my tongue.

I don't look away as I swallow him, power flowing down and in and through. I feel it happen.

The threads of magic that were drawn towards each other like magnets fuse. His magic flows into me and settles in my chest, behind my breastbone. At the same time, I feel a little piece of my magic disappear into him. And in its place I feel an echo right where that magic is settled.

Awe.

Pleasure.

Love.

Gratitude.

Neither Aeric nor I have looked away. Those are his emotions that I'm feeling like reflections. Present but separate. Tinged with the flavor of his magic, and so rightly settled in my mind I wonder how I lived without this knowledge of him.

Through the bond I can sense that he feels the same. There's no thoughts, just the shape of things and emotions. But I also feel that I could put through words. If I tried.

Aeric pulls himself from my lips and lifts me off the floor in one swift motion into his arms. The tears I've had to keep fighting back this morning overflow. Not from sadness, but from the overwhelming relief and love I feel from Aeric.

Stretching me out on the bed, he's suddenly kissing my skin—kissing any part of me that he can reach and roaming with his hands. I feel his intention: to show me exactly how deep his love is. That he wants to give me selfless pleasure back. To savor me.

"Aeric." I pull him back to where we were before, with our faces close and his comforting weight on me. "Just hold me."

"I want to make you moan, Kari. I want to feel you come."

"You will," I whisper, letting him feel what I'm feeling. "I want that too. But for a little while, I just want to feel how this feels."

He rolls to the side, cradling me against his chest. I can feel his contentment and satisfaction, and underlying it all, his happiness. *I love you.* I send the words as clearly as I can through this new space that connects me forever to him.

He doesn't have to speak to send it back, the feeling ringing so deep and so true that I won't ever forget it.

CHAPTER THREE

AERIC

My mate. My mate. My mate.

My heart seems to beat with those two words. I can *feel* her. Like her own heart is fluttering next to mine. It's overwhelming, sensing her emotions like they're my own. And all I can think is *Thank you*.

Inside, I lift those words up like an offering from the Goddess. Right now I don't care that I'm not her only mate, and I even though I know I will still struggle, my perspective has changed. She is irrevocably mine. The fact that she also belongs to others doesn't change that.

Tracing my fingers down the side of her ribs, I feel her shiver under my hand, and I feel the way desire uncurls in her, wanting more. Wanting me. "This is going to take some getting used to," I murmur.

"Yeah."

She's staring at me like she doesn't quite believe I'm real, and I'm right there with her. None of this feels real. But I'm going to take my time making sure that it is. "I want you in my bed tonight," I say.

Kari grins, and her eyes sparkle. "I'm in your bed now. Doesn't that count?"

I cover her body with mine, feeling the little gasp of breath that escapes her when she feels how aroused I am. Again. "It counts. But I want more."

"Yes," she breathes. "Yes."

Slipping my hand beneath her neck, I tighten my fingers just enough to make her eyes go wide. "And this?" I ask.

Kari's cheeks tinge pink with a blush, but she nods. "With you… it feels right."

Satisfaction and pride expand in my chest. That more feral, more fae part of me is reveling in the fact that she feels safe enough with me to let go. To have me take control. But more than that, she's right. The magic that flows between us is far more powerful when we slip into those roles.

"When we're alone," I say. "You're mine."

I let the statement hang between us, waiting for her answer. I want her to say yes. But even if she said no, it wouldn't change a thing. Kari is my mate. Forever.

She doesn't speak for a while, still looking dazed and hazy and content. She uses the tips of her fingers to trace my jaw and then my lips.

"What will that mean?" her voice is soft. "If I yield to you?"

Something about the way she says it—about the word yield—tugs at my gut.

"Nothing more or less than that," I say. "When you're in my bed, I'm the one in charge. You know I would never do anything against your will. I can't."

"I know."

"Do you have a problem with me tying you down and making you scream, and then doing it again, just because I can?"

Kari bites her lip while she turns crimson. "No."

"Good," I say, kissing her softly. "Like I said, I don't belong to the Court of Dominance for a reason. I don't want you to be my submissive. I don't want to give you orders to clean or rules about what you can wear or where you can sit or what you can call me. All I want is you to be mine to pleasure, however I decide that pleasure should take form. And if that means that I get a little more use out of the posts on my bed, so be it." I can't help the smirk on my face.

She rolls her eyes, but I can feel in that space—that's colored pale blue and violet, just like her magic—that she's also amused. And then she smiles at me. "You know, I'm glad for more than just the bond."

"What do you mean?"

It's her turn to smirk, and the sultry way she lifts her hips into mine sends me straight to a place of desire. "I mean that now there's one less cock I have to avoid out of sheer temptation to lick it. Especially now that I know that you taste like your magic."

I laugh. One that shakes free from my chest and rings through the room. "What does my magic taste like?"

I feel her surprise and confusion. "You don't know?"

"To me it's just my power. I never thought about what it might feel like to someone else. And I've never had anyone comment about its flavor." The shy giggle that escapes her lodges in my chest. I'm going to remember that sound forever, and spend my life trying to get her to repeat it. "Tell me."

Kari shakes her head. "I don't want to now." The emotions I feel from her tell me that she's teasing. Testing. Flirting.

I reach out with magic, knowing that I can tease her into telling me. It's easy to draw the tendril of power down her spine, and I savor the way she wiggles underneath me. "Tell me."

"What if it's wrong?"

I chuckle. "If it's the way it feels to you, how is that wrong?"

She scrunches up her nose. "I hate it when you

make good points. But now I'm wondering if the same magic feels or tastes different to different people."

"I honestly couldn't tell you."

Kari runs her palms along my shoulders. "Sometimes you're mint. Sometimes it's like Christmas—cinnamon and nutmeg. Sometimes it's cardamom. But it's always spices. Always green. Refreshing."

"That doesn't sound too bad."

She shakes her head. "It's not. I love it." I can feel her hesitance before she speaks again, a little friction in that space inside that's now reserved for her. And when she speaks I know why. I'm the one that put that friction there. "I love all of your magics," she says softly. "You're all so different."

My hand is still on her neck, and I lift her face to mine, taking her lips in a kiss before I whisper. "I'm sorry, Kari. I know I already said it but I'll say it again. "Don't be afraid to talk about the others with me. It's my problem, and I'm the one who has to overcome it. But this," I say, pushing the emotion of our bond towards her. "This helps."

"I'm glad," she says. "I hoped that it would. And fuck it feels amazing," she laughs.

"I feel you here." I push up so I can touch the space next to my physical heart. "And I'd never thought of magic as having a flavor, but I understand what you mean when you say it has color."

Kari's face lights up. "Do I have one?"

I nod. Finding the words to describe something like this isn't easy. "It's pale blue and purple. Like the color of human forget-me-nots, but made of light and heat."

"That's pretty. It's that color for me too, like the blue at the base of a flame. And the Goddess's magic is all shimmer and gold."

I chuckle. "That makes sense."

It's amazing how even breathing feels different now. Because every breath now reverberates between us. And even though her magic is more color than taste, I love the way Kari actually tastes, and I never have enough.

"Tonight," she says. "I look forward to that."

"I think we can start right now." I sink down her body, soaking in the feeling of her pleasure echoing in my chest. It's like having a brand new road map to her body, and I think I'm going to like memorizing the ways I can wring pleasure out of every part of her.

Her body purrs and stretches when I trace the lines of her hips. A place to come back to. I'm so close to tasting her that my mouth is watering. In the same way that I can feel her pleasure, she can feel my desire—the all-consuming need to have the taste of sugar on my tongue.

When I reach her she's already wet. Glistening. Gorgeous and delicious. The sound Kari makes as I seal my mouth over her sends arousal shooting through me, and I don't think any blood is left in my head. It's all in my cock. The taste of her only makes it better.

A discordant jangling of magic hits me in the chest, and I spring off the bed in one motion, instinct tearing me away from Kari. That was one of my wards echoing, like a hole had been ripped through it. But reaching out, it doesn't seem damaged.

"Aeric?" Kari's looking at me, confused and worried.

I hear the ringing sound of steel from elsewhere in the house, and raised voices. "Aeric! We need you."

That was Kent, knowing I would hear. Shit. Shit. Shit. I pull on my pants and grab the sword that I trained with this morning. "Stay here," I tell Kari, though even as I'm running down the stairs I know that there's no way in hell that she's going to listen to that.

CHAPTER FOUR

KARI

*W*hat the hell? One minute Aeric's mouth is on me and the next he's leaping off me like I suddenly have the plague. Something happened that I either couldn't hear or didn't notice, and the only clothes I had in here are lying in shreds on the floor.

I can hear voices from downstairs, and they don't sound happy. But I haven't heard any screaming or maiming yet either. If he thinks that I'm not going to come see what's going on, he's out of his mind. No, I'm not fae, and no, I don't have the years of fighting experience that my mates have. But I'm not the helpless girl I was either—not when I have Cerys's magic burning in my veins.

Quickly, I slip into my room and pull on some clothes—leggings and a shirt that's within reach—before hurrying down to the main hall. My shield is firmly in place, and I pull up magic from the well in order to make it thicker.

The scene when I round the corner makes me freeze. The men are spread in a loose circle in surrounding the main entrance, except for Brae. Brae has Kiaran up against a pillar, a wickedly long knife pressed against his throat. And he's not pressing it gently either.

"Told you," Aeric mutters when I appear, and I just catch Kent rolling his eyes. In spite of myself I smirk. They know me too well.

Urien looks at me. "Seems he was here after all. But I have no idea how he walked through the wards."

I look at Kiaran, and his eyes are locked on mine. We both know why, but he's not stupid, and claiming to be my mate right now would only get him a knife through the throat. "I have a message for Kari, from Ariana. I'm not here to hurt her or take her. I may have gotten through the wards but you damn well know there's no way I can get her out past them."

"Let him go," I say softly.

Kent steps to my side. "I'm not so sure that's a good idea."

I look at Kent and raise an eyebrow. "We're surrounding him, have him inside wards, and he has no element of surprise. You think there's no way the six of us couldn't contain him if he tries anything?"

Brae chuckles, but takes a step back. He doesn't relax his stance or put away his knife, but at least

Kiaran has a little breathing room. "What's the message?" I ask.

"It's only for you. Not them."

Verys laughs softly. "Not on your life."

I watch Kiaran's hands fold into fists, and I can tell he's trying to restrain himself. Instinct—or the magic possessing him—is telling to fight back. But he won't. Whether it's because he's my mate or because of my magic, I know that he's telling the truth. That reality is sitting deep in my gut. "Yes, Verys."

He turns and looks at me with shock. All of them would if they weren't so intent on watching Kiaran's every move. Honestly, given what they currently know, I don't blame them. Aeric's words are practically a snarl. "We're not leaving you with him."

I don't really want to have this argument right now, not in front of Kiaran. I don't know what he will pass back to Ariana against his will. So I step to Aeric's side, and push confidence and ease through our bond to counteract the anger and fear he's currently projecting towards me. And I like that I can feel his fear. Because I know that's what's driving him. Not wanting to ever risk losing me again.

I speak so softly that I know no one but him will be able to hear me. "We've had no clue about her intentions and now she's sending us a message. I need to hear it, and he's not going to give it to me unless we're alone. We've got him trapped. I know you don't like it, but this has to happen. Test my shield if you're that worried."

Immediately, there're tingles of pale green magic scattered across the surface of the shield, testing and pressing. And in my chest I feel his grudging resignation, that this is the only choice.

"You can take it out on me later," I tell him, unable to resist adding a smile.

I can feel the flare of his arousal, even though nothing changes on the outside. "Verys, Brae," he says. "Outside the front. The rest of us will go out the back."

There's a moment of hesitation before any of them move, but Aeric nods to them, and they slowly go. I'm sure he'll be telling them what I said. I'm right, even if their instincts are screaming. Hell, my instincts are screaming too. Kiaran is dangerous, even if he is my mate. He's powerful as hell, and if he changed his mind about what he wanted to try, I might not be able to stop him.

That's a risk that I have to take.

I wait until they're all out of sight and then some. They're probably listening, but I keep my voice as quiet as possible. They'll know what they need to know soon enough. Kiaran relaxes once they disappear, crouching down and running a hand through his hair before standing and pacing.

"Coming here like this was stupid. You know that right?"

"And they should know that trying to kill me is just as foolish."

I cross my arms. "They're not going to kill you."

"The knife at my throat had me fooled."

Pulling in the range of my shield so that it's closer to my body, I take a step towards him. "Why did she send you?"

His face changes when I come near. Confusion and then pain. Kiaran's body goes rigid, and then he looks at me. Jaw tight, his voice is almost strangled. "I can only remember sometimes."

My stomach drops to my toes. "Remember what?"

Kiaran shudders, groaning. "Who you are to me." He snaps back into that easy posture that I recognize, eyes lit with too much shine. It's easy for me to tell when it's not him. I can see the power and the mania that lies behind him when she's in control. "You have one week, to come to her, and surrender yourself. At the house where you set the ambush."

I hesitate, pulled in between two different desires. I want to push her magic away and see the real Kiaran. I want to tell him that it's all right. But I also know the last time we met that she would never stop, and if I don't get enough information from him, I may never be able to truly see him.

"One week or what?"

The smile that comes across his face chills me to the bone, because it looks like her. "Or she will take your life apart piece by piece. If she can't have the magic you currently possess, she will kill your mates and take it from them to accomplish her goals. Everything you love in this world will be taken from you, until none of them are left. And after you have nothing left, she'll still come for you, because you have what she wants."

Goosebumps rise on my skin. I can almost hear her voice saying it to Kiaran in my head. The very particular wording of it. *Until none of them are left.* My mates. Everything to me and who I am now.

I can hear her coolly and calmly declaring her intention to murder and torture. The ghost of pain and her magic surge over my skin, and I have to take a step back. Take a breath.

I can feel Aeric's worry at the same time that I sense he's trying to project calm. I latch onto that. Imagine my mates' hands on my skin so they're grounding me the same way that they did in New York when I had my flashback. Slowly, air seeps into my lungs that doesn't taste of orange and ash. "Why?" I ask him.

"Why what?" It's his turn to take a step forward, and he does, pressing himself up against my shield so I can feel him and his power. I should feel threatened. I don't. I feel longing.

I don't have to hear the Goddess's voice to choose this time. Inch by inch, I shrink the shield until it's flush with my skin. Kiaran moves with it, until we're separated by nothing but scraps of magic. "Don't pretend you don't understand the question," I tell him, desperately trying to ignore the fact that I want to drop the shield.

"Why does Ariana want you to surrender yourself?" His smirk is wicked. "I'm not allowed to tell you that. It's a surprise."

Focusing, I imagine the golden, glowing shield that's covering my body. I need to do this fast. I form a hole that's just big enough, and push my hand through, catching Kiaran's and winding our fingers together.

It takes him by surprise, and the hiss of pain he lets out is followed by the manic, glittering light leaving his eyes. Kiaran takes a deep, shuddering breath. "Kari."

"I'm sorry," I say, releasing his hand. "I don't want to hurt you."

"*No*," he says quickly, grasping my hand. "Don't let go. The pain helps keep me here."

The magic between us evaporates like it knows that I'm safe and that we need each other more than a shield, and then his mouth is on mine, followed by his groan of pain. He pulls back an inch, just far enough to speak and not far enough to let go. "She wants to remake the world," Kiaran says. "Entirely. Completely. From scratch. And she needs you to do it."

"How?"

He shakes his head. "I don't know. She hasn't told me that." I hesitate, unsure whether to believe him, but he grabs my arms, and I feel the sweep of blue magic from my dreams. "I swear it."

"I believe you."

This time his kiss is soft. Wandering. What a first kiss might feel like—testing the waters of something that's new and precious. It resonates through my soul like a bell and leaves me aching for what we're missing. I have to save him. I have to. That pull towards him is like a tide rushing outward—a yearning that I don't have the power or desire to resist.

He shudders again, and suddenly his hand is on my throat. That manic glint is back in his eyes, and dread pools in the base my stomach along with pure, icy, terror. She's back, and he didn't even have time to warm me. Kiaran's mouth twists in an ugly smile, dark hair falling into his eyes. "One week, Kari, and I'll see you again." His fingers twitch tighter for a moment, and I see conflict in his expression before he turns and releases me. He strides out the front entrance without looking back. As if he didn't just kiss me with a tenderness that I can still feel.

It's like I don't exist to him.

Right now, maybe I don't.

Fuck.

I lean against the same pillar that Brae had him cornered against and sink down to the floor. I guess the ball is in our court now. At least partially.

"He's gone," Brae says, coming inside. "Portaled out as soon as he was clear of the wards."

"Okay," I say. They're going to ask how he got through, and I'm going to have to tell them. Because I can't have them kill him the next time that we see each other, which might be in a week.

Aeric's echoes reverberate in my chest, coming into focus again and growing more powerful as he strides in from outside. Relief seeing me whole and unharmed. Anxiety over some of the things that he felt from me. Resolve that he's going to try to keep his instincts in check. But when he comes over to me and picks me up off the floor, I don't resist. It feels right, like a little missing piece of me is back with him touching me.

I wonder if that's the way I'll feel with all of them? Like something is missing unless they're close. I both love that and at once am terrified of it. But it's the good kind of terrified—like standing on a cliff over a crashing sea. More awe and wonder and reverence than actual fear.

Everyone gathers together while Aeric tucks me against his side. "Let's start with how much you overheard," I say.

"Not much," Verys says. His face isn't happy. "And I'd rather start with why you forced us out of there."

I search his face, surprised that this is coming from him. "Nothing happened." It hits me as I watch him. Kiaran is the one who almost killed him, and he swore to me that he would step in front of me as many times as he was able. I took away his option to do that, and with the person that nearly cost him his life. "I'm sorry, Verys. We needed to know what he had to say."

"We could have made him talk."

I can only imagine the ways that they would think of to do that, and I stop my horror from leaking out before Aeric can truly sense it. Not to mention the fact that I don't want Kiaran hurt. He's already in enough pain. "That's not who we are."

Verys crosses the distance between us, kneeling in front of me. "Don't make me do that again. Don't make me abandon you."

No one else in the room speaks, and neither do I. The air is clear and still like the break of dawn in winter. This moment, between him and I, is important. I lean forward so that Aeric is no longer touching me, and take Verys's face in my hands. "I would never ask that, Verys. You didn't abandon me. If something had happened, you would have been by my side in a second. Trust the shield you taught me to use."

He presses his face into my stomach, arms coming around me to hold me close, fingers digging into my skin like the thought of letting go is unbearable. "You dropped the shield," he murmurs, so low only I can hear.

I didn't realize that he would be watching for that, and now his terror makes sense. He thought I was not only alone with Kiaran, but defenseless, and I had stopped him from protecting me. I lift his face and kiss him softly. "I was safe. I promise. I'll tell you why I dropped the shield, I swear. But we need to talk about this first."

Verys doesn't move away, just to the side where his hand can curl possessively around my calf. Aeric hauls me back against him, locking his arm around my waist, and I try to suppress my grin, and fail. I end up looking at Kent, who meets me with his own barely contained smile. We both see the territorial nature of Aeric's movement.

I should say that I don't like it. That I can't believe that this many men want to be with me and have a hard time keeping their hands off me. But I can't say that, because I love it. And after sealing my bond with Aeric, I think he's entitled to a small dose of possessiveness.

I clear my expression. Unfortunately, the laughter can't be a part of this discussion. "He said that I have one week."

"For what?" Brae asks.

"To surrender myself to Ariana. The meeting place is the house in the Crystal Court where we set the trap."

Urien laughs. "Well, clearly we're not going to do that."

"It could be an opportunity to set a trap that will actually work," Kent counters.

"She'll have people there now, watching and waiting in case we do exactly that," Urien says. "She's been one step ahead of us in every way, and if she's setting up a meeting we can be sure that she already has about a hundred contingency plans."

Verys clears his throat. He doesn't look happy,

but a little calmer at least. "I heard you ask why. Did he tell you?"

I press my lips together, anxiety bubbling in my gut. How do I tell them why he told me? "He said that she wants to remake the world. Entirely, completely, and from scratch. And that she thinks she needs my magic—which I assume means the Goddess's magic—to do it." No one speaks, the air heavy with sudden unspoken meaning. "Okay, I thought it was weird but clearly that means something different to you than it means to me."

"How would she do that?" Aeric asks. "*Could* she do it?"

Brae shakes his head. "I have no idea. With enough power, maybe it's possible? But the magic that guards Allwyn is incredibly powerful. It's a long shot if anything."

"What are you talking about?" I ask.

"What you just said," Verys answers, "is what Cerys did when she sacrificed herself to remake Allwyn and free it from the old gods."

I rub my hands over my face before pressing my temples to alleviate the oncoming headache from trying to wrap my head around this. "You're saying she wants to destroy Allwyn and put it back together? Why would she want that?"

"Maybe that's not what she meant," Aeric says, rubbing a hand on my back.

"I don't know. He did not explain." He didn't have *time* to explain.

Brae stands. "Maybe it's not quite literal. But I agree with Urien, we shouldn't go."

"We have to go," I say, holding up a hand before they can say anything. "Obviously I'm not going to surrender—we'll figure that part out. But she threatened to kill every one of you if I don't do this."

"I'd like to see her try," Aeric says in a low voice.

I spin to look at him. "I wouldn't. Ariana has stolen magic before, obviously. We have no idea how much she's taken and who from. It's clear she can control fae, so let's not pretend this isn't a real threat."

Aeric pulls me back against his chest, closer. The fierceness of emotion I feel through our bond takes my breath away. He doesn't say anything, just places his lips on my skin and it's enough. They know it's a threat—of course they do—and they'll fight like hell to make sure that doesn't happen.

Urien clears his throat. "Should we tell the Rialoi? Or the Crystal Court. It's on their territory."

"Maybe," Brae admits. "But we should come up with a plan of action first. Assess everything. We don't want them sending fae into a situation we don't understand."

Kent crosses his arms. "Any ideas on a plan?"

"I wish I could say yes." Brae shakes his head. "But right now? No."

"We should go back and see if she's already laid traps," Verys says.

"It's a good idea." I'm not even sure who says it, because I feel that same simple touch of magic that I felt this morning. Blue like the depths of the sea—fingers grazing down my cheek. I don't feel like I can sit here and figure out this plan. Restlessness itches under the surface of my skin and something pulling me away.

I stand. "I'm sure you'll figure something out. I need a minute."

As I follow the tug in my gut I note that I need to stop walking away from them in the middle of important conversations. But I've never felt this kind of draw before, and it doesn't feel like it's from the Goddess or even Kiaran. This is subtle. Almost like a faint breeze or following a scent.

All of our rooms are on the second floor, branching off of the balcony that surrounds the mansion's central courtyard. My room is on the left at the top of the stairs, large enough that it's the only entrance on that side of the rectangle. And the other five rooms are arrayed around the rest of it. But something looks different, like the dimensions have shifted a bit.

My gut drops when I see it.

There are now seven doors on this floor instead of six. On the far side, where there were only two rooms, there are now three. And I realize that it's the house that's guiding me, pulling me towards the room in the middle.

I've never seen this room before. In fact, I doubt that it existed before now. But even though I've never seen it before, I recognize it. As if I needed another confirmation, the house has made it real. This is where the magic of this home has chosen to house my mates, and this room belongs to Kiaran.

CHAPTER FIVE

KARI

The room in front of me is beautiful. Somehow walking the line between stark and delicate. The walls are the pale grey of a sunrise shrouded in mist, and furnishings that don't match. Almost as if the things had washed up on the shore of a beach and been rescued. These rooms reflect the deepest desires of those they provide for —to provide the sense of peace and safety that we subconsciously crave.

Though Kiaran has been here before, this is the first time he set foot in the house. And the magic sensed what none of the others have been able to. There will be no hiding it now, and they need to know.

At the back of the room is a pool that spills out and leads to the garden, just as it does in my room. But this pool is bigger and deeper, the blue disappearing down into depths that I can't see. How much can magic play with the laws of space and physics here? I'm not sure. But I'm willing to bet that if I went below this room downstairs there would be no sign of a pool that reaches infinite depths.

There are also small foundations and one of the walls has water trickling down it one smooth curtain, nearly silent and beautifully smooth. The air in the room is rich with moisture, but not overpowering. Feels like being at the beach. I wonder what the beaches of Allwyn are like. Are they packed with souls looking for an escape too, like they are in the human world?

I sit down at the end and put my feet in, the temperature cool and perfect. If only this were simple. Kiaran has attacked me multiple times. Attacked my other mates. I shouldn't want him the way I do. And yet…I can't imagine abandoning him any more than the others. He's a part of me already.

Swirling my feet in the water, I sigh. I need to tell them, and I need to do it now. I can't let them find this room on their own. It will hurt enough without that.

I reach out through my bond with Aeric. *Come. Everyone.*

Not totally sure that exact words will go through, but I hope that he understands the shape of it. It's only a few minutes until I hear the sounds of footsteps on the stairs, and I resist turning around until I hear them at the door.

If the looks on all of their faces didn't tell me that they understood, then the pang of pain and panic that I feel from Aeric would have told me. "I'm sorry," I say. "I didn't know how to tell you."

"How long have you known?" It's Kent's question as he steps through the door. The rest of them spread out, looking a bit uncomfortable, but taking it in stride. Aeric is the one that won't step through.

Until he looks at me. I smile, trying to tell him that I'm sorry and that I love him with a look. Finally, he walks forward and sits beside me. Nobody comments on his hesitation, which I'll have to thank them for later.

"Since after the first attack. When I was outside in the gardens before he appeared, I got sick enough that I thought I was going to throw up. And then everything happened. I didn't realize what it meant until later, and when I went to see the Goddess, she confirmed that the number was six. Not five."

"Six," Kent murmurs. "That means—"

"Yeah." I reach out for his hand, and he takes it. "You're meant to be here too."

Urien is the first one to question. "If he's your mate too, then why is he still with Ariana?"

"He's under her control," I explain. "Though I'm not exactly sure how. He can break free for moments at a time, which is why I dropped my shield when he was here. It was only the free Kiaran that told me that she wants to remake the world. When she's in control he can't say it, and he doesn't always remember who I am."

Brae still looks stunned. "This explains why you didn't want me to kill him."

"And why he left without taking you from the trap," Verys adds. "This changes everything."

I cover my face with my hands. "I know, and I know it was wrong not to tell you but I didn't know how. After what happened to you," I gesture at Verys, "and at the house. Everything. I just—I'm sorry. I'll say it as many times as you need me to, and I'll take what you throw at me."

Kent rolls his eyes.

"What?"

"Sure, you should have told us, Kari. But it's not like you asked for another mate any more than you asked for the first four. I wish I'd known, but I'm not angry at you."

"You should be," I say softly.

Brae raises an eyebrow. "Would that make you feel better? For us to berate you for not telling us something because you were afraid of our reaction to the news? If anything we should be apologizing to you for feeling that you had to keep anything from us."

There're murmurs of agreement from everyone. "Especially me," Aeric whispers.

"You all are too nice," I say, tucking my head into Aeric's shoulder, and Verys laughs. "We'll keep it in mind to be meaner to you."

"You know what I mean."

Urien clears his throat and his eyes are hard. "We do. And I don't want to be the one to say it, but I will. Mate or not, if he tries to kill you, we will defend you. If he tries to kill us, we will defend ourselves."

I nod, pulling my feet out of the seemingly infinite pool and standing. "I want a way to free him."

"Well, this definitely gives more of a reason to go to the meeting. If he's present maybe I can get more of an idea of how the magic is affecting him."

"Did you guys have any other ideas?"

They shake their heads. "Not unless you count 'under no circumstances are you surrendering yourself,'" Kent says.

"Right."

"I'm going to the Crystal Court to check out the spot," Brae says.

"We're going to check everywhere," Kent says. "Over the next few days. Everywhere we've been to see if she's been following. New York, checking on

Emma and Odette. Lunar Court. Everywhere in Carnal."

"If we feel even a shred of her magic, it might give us more insight."

I could easily argue against it, but they're right, but I don't feel like pressing them right now. "Be careful, please. All of you."

Brae smirks as he pulls me close to kiss me. "I'm always careful."

"People in the human world say that just before bad things happen."

"I will be back before you know it," he whispers in my ear.

Kent salutes me before he leaves the room, and Verys kisses my forehead quickly. I'm left with Urien and Aeric, unsure about what to do. Now there's a ticking clock hanging over us, but I can't take any action. I hate that.

When I look up from where I've been staring at the marble tiles, Urien has faded away, and Aeric is looking at me with some of that fire from earlier. I can feel the intensity of his desire in my chest, and it kindles my own.

He steps to me, raising my eyes to his. "You're frustrated," he says.

"Yes."

"You want to do something?"

I sigh. "Of course. I'm fucking tired of being in limbo. Why a week? Why does she want to wait? Let's do it now, get it out of the way. Maybe *that's* the element of surprise we need. Have Brae track Kiaran through the portal and lets just show up."

He raises a dark eyebrow. "And what would we do when we got there?"

"I don't know." The need to move and break and do *something* slithers under my skin like a menace.

Aeric does what he did earlier, slipping his hand behind my neck and gripping just hard enough to get my attention—just hard enough to send liquid heat sliding down my spine where it gathers low in my belly.

"I know you want to do something. I do too. But diving in without a plan is dangerous. For everyone. In the meantime, I'm sure we can find something to occupy your…interests."

I have an idea of what he's thinking, and right now I'm very much on board with this distraction. "What did you have in mind?"

Aeric's eyes are hard with dominance and command. "You will come to my room when fade begins. Do what you need to do before then, because you will be mine—and no one else's—until bright comes again."

Mating night. That's only fair. "Okay. Should I… do anything special to get ready?"

"Don't wear anything that you don't want destroyed," he says.

I can do that.

Excited, fizzy, nerves sparkle in my stomach as I stand in front of the door to Aeric's bedroom. It's shut, and I haven't seen him since he left me standing in Kiaran's room, staring after him and impossibly aroused. But his command did exactly what he intended. It turned me on while giving me something to focus on besides the fact that an evil fae wants to steal my goddess-given magic to destroy the world.

It's a hard thing not to think about, but I wasn't able to sink into a spiral of worry and despair while I was going through the immense amount of lingerie in my closet. Kaya has given me way too much, but if my mates are going to be in the habit of tearing it off me, maybe it's a good amount. Next time I see her I'm going to have to ask her if she foresaw a lot of her creations ending up in tatters.

In the end I selected red. A dark one that's almost crimson. I think it will go well with Aeric's red walls, and the almost see-through, silky material of the bra and panties makes my skin pop. I feel good in this, and if he does in fact destroy it, I can ask Kaya for more like it. Hell, she'd probably make me one in every color if I asked her.

I don't exactly know what to expect from Aeric, other than sex. This powerful side of him is new, and exploring it makes me as jittery and timid as it does hot and bothered. But from Aeric—in that place that's now reserved only for him—I've felt only calm and contentment. Even now, that's all I feel.

Softly, I knock on the door. I hear footsteps inside, and Aeric opens the door. He's wearing dark pants with no shirt, the contrast making the darker patterns on his skin stand out. There's only been a handful of moments where I've literally lost my breath because something was so beautiful, and this is one of them.

"Hi." The word is more breath than voice.

He takes my hand and pulls me into the space, and even though I was just here earlier it feels completely different. Dark curtains are pulled across the windows and candles make the space glow with sensual light. Just that simple change makes the space darker and sexier. The walls feel like they've become a deeper red and I swear that I can feel my heart pounding in every part of my body.

"You're nervous," he says.

Obviously he can feel it. "A little."

"Why?" It's not a criticism but a genuine question. "It's just me."

"It feels different."

Aeric walks over to the dark wooden table where there's two glasses of wine and a spread of cheese, fruit, and other things. He brings one of the glasses of wine to me. "It's just us," he says again. "Experimenting. Seeing what works."

That's true. I take the glass from him and look at the golden liquid. It seems to shimmer in the glass like a thousand galaxies are swirling inside it. "I've only had Fae mead. Never wine. You know there are rumors about what happens to humans who drink Fae wine."

Aeric chuckles, low and warm, and lifts his own glass to his lips. "It won't do anything to you that human wine wouldn't."

The taste as it hits my tongue is incredible. Fruity and sweet with layers of sugar and spice and none of the bitterness of human wine. But I can feel the way it swims in my veins and head right away. "I think it's probably a bit stronger."

"Yes." I feel his intention change as he reaches for me. "Come here." I do, letting him loop his arms around my waist and pull me close. "I want to make sure you're all right with this," he says. "And that you understand that no answer can or will change anything between us."

Slowly, I shift so I can take one more heady sip of wine before raising my gaze to his. I'm used to being in control. Of taking charge. I had to as a dancer, when I opened the shop, and even now it drives me crazy that I can't do more to fix whatever is happening around us. But like I told him this morning, with him it feels easy and right.

It's a hard thing to put my finger on. But all of this—him, the other guys, the Goddess, all of it—is not something that I thought I would have wanted. And it only makes sense that my relationship with every one of my mates is different and unique. That I give myself to Aeric completely when I'm in his bed clicks on a level so deep that I don't think I could find it if I tried.

"I want to explore this with you," I tell him finally. "Because in the same way that I can't unravel why I've been given this many mates—or mates at all —this feels..." I slip my free hand between us to rest on my stomach. "It almost...resonates. Right here."

Aeric leans down and drops a kiss on my shoulder. "Yes."

Taking the glass of wine away from me, he spins me towards the bed and walks with me to it. Though his hands are still around my waist and he's leaning so his chin rests on my shoulder. Through our bond I feel anticipation and curiosity. And then I see why.

On the bed in front of me are strips of dark green leather. Such a dark jade that I nearly think it's just an inky black. The lengths of them vary, and I see holes and buckles like a belt. I know enough about the kinky side of sex to know what they're for, and my heart starts to hammer in my chest. "Is that what you bought?" I ask.

"Hmm?"

"When we went to the sex store in New York, is this what you bought?"

His low laughter vibrates up my spine. "No, these I made. For you."

"You made these?" I say, reaching out to touch the leather. It's soft and smooth, the underside lined with even softer materials. "When?"

A graze of teeth on the side of my neck that brings goosebumps to the surface. "While you were picking out this red thing that's driving me mad."

I arch back into him. "I'm glad you like it. But seriously? You made these *today*? Where did you learn?"

Aeric laughs again. "I know how to do lots of things." His voice lowers. "And just because I am not a member of the Court of Dominance does not mean that I have not spent time there."

Oh. That's where he learned.

I play my hand on two of the much longer strips. "What are these for?"

"It would be easier to show you," he says, smiling into my skin.

"Okay."

Coming from behind me, Aeric picks up the first of the leather cuffs and reaches for my wrist. He wraps it around my arm with slow yet deliberate tenderness, and I shiver. It fits perfectly—secure, but not too tight. And it looks sexy. The other wrist is cuffed, and then he moves to my ankles, placing kisses onto my thighs while he buckles them on. When he stands again he's smirking in that devastatingly sexy way. "On the bed."

He catches one of my wrists as I settle in the center against the pillows, and then he's threading black rope through the metal ring on the cuff. Rope attached to his bed posts that I didn't even notice when I walked in. The way he ties the knot is smooth and efficient. Like he's done it a hundred times before.

Maybe he has.

And when I test my arm against it, there's no

give. It's not uncomfortable, but there's no getting out. No escape. But I don't want to get out of this.

My other arm bound to the opposite post, Aeric joins me on the bed, settling on his knees in-between my legs. Casually, he runs a hand down my chest, over the lingerie, just to show me that he can.

"I could have taken these off," I say, trying to keep my voice steady.

"And deny me the fun of tearing them off you? No." He smiles down at me, "And this is what these are for."

The long strip of leather is in his hand, and he wraps it around my thigh, cinching the buckle tight. And then the other one. I swallow. "I've never seen those before."

I can feel amusement from him as he unravels another length of rope. "They come in handy." The rope is tied to the cuff just like my wrists, and I gasp when he loops it around the bedpost where my wrist is secured and pulls, stretching my leg up and out. It's very clear what they're for now. I'll be completely exposed and open for him.

The surge of arousal that goes through me makes me close my eyes, and I feel like I'm sinking into the feeling. "I thought you might like this," he murmurs, binding my other leg.

Aeric settles over me, the hardness of his cock

right up against me where I desperately need it. But the look on his face tells me he knows that he has all the time in the world. After all, there's nothing I can do to make him move faster. Except maybe beg.

That thought and the subtle rocking of his hips make me go blind with desire. "Woah."

"There it is," he says, kissing me softly. "Let it all go."

I'm shaking with adrenaline and need and I try to lift up my hips to meet his, but I have no leverage. "Is this what you thought about when we were in the crystal court?" I ask. "When you held me down and used your mouth on me?"

Aeric's voice is a rich whisper against my lips, and in the warm light of all the candles his face is full of love, lust, and truth. "I was mainly concerned with keeping you alive," he says. "But if I told you that the thought didn't cross my mind I would be a liar."

"Is it like you thought it would be?"

"Much, much better."

He rocks his hips again, and I moan. "You're going to kill me."

"Little deaths only."

I laugh and it turns to nothing but air when he runs his fingers over the fabric of my panties. "Very clever." There's a French phrase that means *the little death* that is often used to mean orgasms. Or in Aeric's case, lots and lots of orgasms.

"I try." He strokes over me again, and I instinctively pull at the restraints, wanting more. "You know what I like about this position?" He asks softly.

I shake my head.

"There are so many possibilities. I could take you here," he brushes his thumb along my lower lip. "And watch you suck my cock while you can't go anywhere."

"You're just saying it like that to turn me on more."

His smile is satisfied. "It's working too."

Dammit, he's right. I'm soaking through my underwear.

"But I can also take you here." Slipping his hand between us, he runs his finger over my clit through the fabric and down to my entrance. "Or even here." Fingers keep moving, brushing over my ass.

"Goddess," I say. "I don't know which one of those sounds better."

He grins, and kisses me hard. "You don't get to choose."

Fuck. I wiggle underneath him, trying to get him to move, or do more. But he's absolutely in control. "While I have you here, Kari, I want to tell you something."

That gets my attention, and I go still. "What?"

"No matter what happens, I will always protect you. I don't give a shit about Ariana's motives or why she thinks she needs you. No one takes my mate away from me. You're mine. And I'm yours." Leaning down, he brushes his lips against my ear. "I'm not letting you go."

The words resonate across the thread that connects us like a bell. For him, this is a vow of loyalty and love. It strikes me directly in my heart, wrapping it in peace and comfort. He lets the moment hang between us for one more moment before he smiles. "One more thing." He reaches out of sight and comes back with a length of silky black cloth. I don't even have a chance to ask him what it's for before he's tying it over my eyes. "Aeric," I say.

"Breathe." The command is simple and short, but I take a breath, relaxing into the sudden darkness as the fabric tightens. Nothing has changed. I can still feel his weight pressing against me, still feel that steadiness he's projecting—even if that's now spun together with his own arousal—and I can still feel that desperate need that I have for him.

The air is so charged between us with lust and magic that I can almost feel Aeric move before he does. When he does move it's with smooth precision. Up my body so he's straddling my chest. I can feel the power in his legs and it only emphasizes my vulnerable position, open for him.

Rustling fabric reaches my ears, and then fingers under my chin. "Open."

I know that he can feel the desire that slams into me like a wave, a pure reaction to the stark command in his voice. The tip of his cock brushes my lips, and I open for him. He tastes just as good as this morning. Like a fucking cinnamon lollipop.

The thought almost makes me giggle, but I'm already too full of him to make a sound. All I can do is suck harder and enjoy. Bon appétit.

Aeric thrusts his hips deeper, and I take as much of him as I can, enjoying that I can just *do* this. We're mated. It's not for any magic purpose but making him feel good. I never thought that being tied up and sucking a cock would turn me on so much that it makes my toes curl, but that's exactly what's happening right now.

Swirling my tongue around his head, I can feel the swell of pleasure from him. He likes that. I do it again, and again, enjoying the echoes of his pleasure building on themselves. He groans above me, and I swear I can hear the wood of the headboard creak under his hands. "I think you're the one that's going to kill me, Kari."

I can only hum around his shaft, moving as much

as I can, bound the way that I am. But he pulls away, swiftly moving so that he can reach my skin, working his way down my body in an echo of how he did this morning before we were interrupted.

Fingers weave under the band of my bra. A flick of magic and it shreds under his hands easily, baring me to him. Only a feather touch of lips before his mouth is on my nipples, tasting one and then the other and back again before he slips down further. I want to reach for him. Hold him against my skin and wordlessly beg for more. But when I reach, I can't. The cuffs keep my arms in place, sending me back into that state of delicious vulnerability, where my only option is to let go and *feel*.

Aeric makes a low sound of pleasure. "I'd better not be interrupted this time."

I don't have a chance to respond. His tongue is on me, directly through my panties, heat and texture already driving me insane. And with my legs held open the way they are, I'm spread like a feast for him.

Magic curls up and into me—the first time that he's used it to touch *me*—igniting a flare of arousal deep in my core. It steals my breath, working both with and against the motion of his tongue, steady and complimentary rhythm bringing me up and to the edge faster than I thought possible. I can feel myself grow even more wet, and Aeric groans. Another tiny flick of that magic and the fabric tears and disappears entirely.

Through the magic of our bond, I can feel the sheer pleasure running through him when he tastes me for real. The echoes of his pleasure build on mine, making it louder and bolder and impossible to ignore. I hope that it's the same for him at the same time that I'm in awe that I can make him feel this way—that I can make anyone feel this way.

Aeric seals his mouth over my clit, sucking with determined ferocity. My hips are rising to meet his mouth as much as they're able and I'm writhing in the restraints. The fact that I can't move somehow makes this better and worse all at once. I can't move or breathe or do anything to hold myself back from going over the edge, and he's determined to send me there.

Until he's not.

He pulls back, both with his magic and with the intensity of his mouth, and the orgasm I was about to have evaporates into mist. I moan, the loss of all that pleasure jarring and frustrating and somehow sexy, because he did it on purpose. "Fucking hell," I say, and he laughs softly, even with his mouth occupied.

"I've got all night," he murmurs. "Can't make it that easy."

"I think you could," I say, lifting my hips as far as they'll go, desperate for him to touch me again, for that cool spicy flow of magic rushing under my skin. He runs his hands up my thighs, and I shiver. "I want to see you," I tell him. "Please."

I blink against the candlelight as he removes the blindfold, and the sight is one that has me half-way back to orgasm. Aeric is sprawled on the bed between my legs, the curve of his ass visible from the trousers slipping down his hips. His mouth is ravishing my clit, the flickering light making his hair almost shimmer and drawing attention to the curling marks on his skin. I'm transfixed, watching him.

Deep, slow pleasure unfurls under his tongue, drawn out with his lips and stoked with the barest hint of magic. Sealing his mouth over my clit, Aeric works me in rhythmic pulls of his mouth that have me moaning and wiggling and if he stops again I'm going to have to beg.

I gasp when one little move of his tongue swirls over a spot that makes me see fire, and because he can feel me, he knows. Spreading his hands over the inside of my thighs, he pushes my legs even wider, locking me in place as he teases that spot. I may as well have kept the blindfold on, because I can't see anything but white. I'm shaking under his tongue, the sharp point of it so close I swear I can almost taste it.

Aeric's magic strokes against mine, tangling it and teasing it and pulling it down into the mess of pleasure he's created, and everything explodes. Ecstasy rolls through me like white-hot flame and I can hear my voices echoing off the walls. The orgasm has me shaking, pulling against the restraints while he doesn't stop, drinking me in until I'm shuddering in the aftermath of pleasure.

I come up gasping to find Aeric's face close to mine. One glance downward tells me that he's naked now. His cock is thick and hard between us, and I want it. So badly that I'm wet all over again.

"Aeric—"

My words are cut off with a kiss. His lips tease mine open as he slowly enters me. It's delicious torture. Too much and not enough all at once. I love feeling what he feels—pleasure and satisfaction so deep that I've never felt the like. It's perfect.

And then he starts to move.

This is the first time he's been inside me like this since we've mated, and I swear to the goddess I feel the bond pull us closer. Like little bits of our souls are tangling together and merging. He's not holding back, slamming into me with a force that's shaking the bed, and I need more.

He kisses me until neither of us can breathe, and when we have to break apart he buries his face in my neck so can still savor my skin. I reach for him, and am stopped by the ropes. I keep forgetting that he has me bound, and every time I'm reminded it pulls me back into that place of contentment and heat. He can fuck me as long as he likes while I'm like this. I am entirely his—just the way he wanted.

It's that thought that cracks me open again, orgasm spiraling up and out and rendering me completely senseless. Rolling waves of sensation crashing over me, and again when I feel Aeric come, both through the bond and the heat spilling inside me. It triggers aftershocks that carry me away into bliss. I'm limp and spent, pinned in place by Aeric's body and his cock.

Pressing a soft kiss to my lips, Aeric starts to untie me. "We're done?"

"Not even close," he says, "but you need a rest from these." He releases my legs first, one and then the other, helping me extend them slowly. They're sore in a good way, and a little stiff. I love the way he massages my hips and thighs—digging in his fingers so that the muscles are forced to relax. He does the same with my arms, checking my wrists and massaging my shoulders before pulling me to him. My back rests perfectly against his chest and he kisses that place where my neck meets my spine. "How do you feel?"

"Good." The response is automatic. "Weird. Amazing. My head is buzzy."

"Being tied up can do that."

Aeric moves his arm across my chest so that I'm nearly welded to him. I wouldn't have it any other way. "I liked it. Will we do that every time?"

Another kiss to the side of my neck, and I arch into it. Even that simple movement, and I can feel him hardening behind me. We're definitely not finished. "Not every time," he says. "I don't need cuffs or rope to restrain you. Not when I have magic. And my hands work just fine."

I remember the way he gripped my arms that night in the Crystal Court. That was just as effective as the cuffs—which are still wrapped around my wrists and ankles—and I don't have any doubt that he'll do it again.

"I like feeling you," I say. I don't need to clarify that I'm talking about the mating bond. He knows.

"Mmm. I like it too. I like knowing exactly what makes you shiver."

A breathy laugh escapes me. "I think you've done a pretty good job figuring that out already."

Aeric slips inside me from behind, the tightness of this position making me gasp. I feel fuller here, almost more taken than I did before. "I think I can do better," he says, dragging his lips along the line of my shoulder. "Like I said before: I've got all night, and I intend to use it to learn exactly how my mate likes to be fucked." He punctuates that word with a deep thrust, and I'm no longer capable of speech.

With his arms locked around me and my legs tangled with his, I do what he's been asking for, and let go completely. Even more than when I was bound in rope. Now I'm bound by *him*, and I yield.

I surrender.

My mate wants to learn every part of me, and I'm going to let him.

CHAPTER SIX

AERIC

"We have to tell her," Kent says.

I'm looking up at the ceiling, and away from this morning's 'offering.' Fingers. I felt it when they hit the wards—so hard that it roused me from sleep. There are five, one for each of us with our name grotesquely carved into it. Brae currently has them wrapped in magic in case there's a curse that accompanies them. Seeing if there's anything we can glean before destroying them completely.

It's the same as the last three days. Threats and more threats. Since Kari's new mate—Kiaran—appeared with that message.

"What is telling her going to do except for upset her?" Verys asks. "This distraction plan is working."

Kent sighs and looks at me. He's right. I can feel Kari, still peacefully sleeping upstairs, content. I'm just as loath to upset her, but she deserves to know. "As much as I'm enjoying the job of distracting her," I say, "Kent is right. We just got over her not telling us something because she was concerned with our reaction. It's stupid of us to turn around and do the same thing. And she's going to figure it out. There's a reason that I've *had* to keep distracting her. You think she hasn't noticed that we're hiding something?"

"None of these are from the same fae," Brae says.

My stomach rolls. Last night it was the carcass of a fae beast, so destroyed that it was nearly unrecognizable. There were smaller animals too—birds like the ones that attacked us, with bloody names. The night after Kari and I mated I woke up in a panic, feeling like the wards were being attacked from all sides. It was that mist that Ariana sent after us, battering against the defenses.

She's sending messages that her threats are real and that we should not ignore them. Not that we would, but it's disconcerting. So far though, there's no sign of her anywhere else. Nowhere we've checked has there been any trace. Not even at the meeting place that she's chosen.

But these gifts are escalating.

I watch as Brae incinerates the fingers with pure, raw flame contained within his magical boundary. So hot that there's nothing left. If Ariana cut the fingers from five fae today, we might be getting more pieces of them tomorrow. "She needs to know," I say again. "There's only so many times I'm going to be able to get her to ignore her instincts. Kari is frustrated, and she doesn't know what to do about it."

Kent smirks. "Good thing she has you."

I roll my eyes.

Verys clears his throat. "We're going to Manhattan right now to check on Kari's friends, and around the areas we were before, just to see if there's anything."

"If there isn't anything there, maybe one of her friends could be another distraction," Urien says.

That could be good, but not as a distraction. "It might help her feel more at ease, but I still think we need to tell her about this."

Kent nods. "Later today. After we get back from New York."

There's an uncomfortable silence before we split up. I get why they don't want to tell her. We're all uncomfortable with Kari's pain. Especially me, since now I'll be able to feel it. But I promised Kari that I would try. And that means doing things that might make me uncomfortable.

"Thanks," Kent says, falling into step with me as I walk over to the breakfast table. "For backing me up."

"You're right," I say. "For once."

He crosses his arms. "Don't give me too much credit, or I'll start not to recognize you."

I laugh, grabbing an apple from the table and biting into it. "Don't get used to it."

"I won't. But I can still kick your ass."

"You can try." Now that Kent has his head out of his ass, I really like him. And it's not lost on me that I acted almost the same as he did the other day. Fuck, I can't believe I'm actually comparing myself to a human. But we have more in common than I thought that we did, and the way he's been challenging me in training has had me more on my game than I've been in decades.

Kent clears his throat. "Can I ask you something?"

I raise an eyebrow. "Sure."

"What's it like?" He hesitates. "Mating."

"I'm not going to give you the details of how we did the ritual. Ask Kari for that."

He rolls his eyes. "Not that. The actual connection. I'm not sure that I'm ever going to get it, and so far you're the only one who's experiencing it. I'm just wondering what it's like."

He's not making a joke or fun of me and Kari. If anything, Kent desires this bond with Kari the most out of all of us, and there's no guarantee he'll ever have it. I know Brae wants to find a way, and I check the surge of possessiveness that floods my system at the thought. But it's getting better.

Through that bond, I reach out towards Kari. Feeling her asleep is even stranger than feeling her when she's awake. The emotions are muted, but it's almost as if I can sense her dreams. But I also feel her sense of safety. Her subconscious is letting her relax because she knows that we're here and we'll do anything to protect her. She doesn't need to know that we've taken to sleeping in shifts so that there's someone always alert, and if she knew she wouldn't be surprised.

Kent is still looking at me expectantly.

I lean against the back of one of our couches, and search for the words to describe it. The way our souls merged together so that she's literally a part of me. "It's hard to describe," I tell him. "I can feel her right now, muted, dreaming. When she's awake…it's just like experiencing your own emotions. But these are quieter, and they feel like *her*."

"It sounds strange," Kent says. "I want that, but I can't imagine it."

I take a bite of the apple, and look at him before speaking again. "I've known about mating bonds forever. You learn about them early here. But even knowing what they are and what they're meant to do, I never would have been able to paint this picture. But now that I've felt it, it's as natural as breathing."

The look on his face isn't one I'm used to seeing on Kent. It's concerned and almost sad. Another similarity between Kent and I...we always show confidence to a fault.

"We're going to try," I tell him.

"I didn't say anything."

I smile before taking a final bite of apple. "You didn't have to."

Kent raises an eyebrow before heading to the door. "Just for that I'm going to kick your ass next time we spar."

"You're perfectly welcome to try." I call after him.

He turns before he disappears. "If it's all clear, should we bring one of Kari's friend's back?"

I shrug. "I think it's a good idea. Since she's become fixated on Kari, Ariana hasn't harmed any other humans that we know of, and she seems more fixated on us than anything else. And even slightly misguided Urien is right. Kari needs someone else to talk to besides the five of us."

"Yeah," he says. "That was my thought. We'll keep you posted."

"Good luck."

Kent pretty much always goes on any runs to New York. Even though he doesn't work for their police force anymore, he knows the city and if anything were to happen he'd have more leverage than we would. Once fae began committing crimes, they constructed cells lined with ash that would keep us in check. The last thing we need is to end up in one right now. But I'm not expecting them to encounter anything on this trip.

Ariana has an agenda, and it's moved beyond the human world. What Kiaran told Kari is disturbing, even if it can't be completely trusted. She's making her moves, and my instinct tells me she's finished in the human world. For now.

Quickly, I sprint back up the stairs to my room, where Kari is still sleeping. The sight of her sprawled across my bed and tangled in the blankets sweeps warmth through me. Her red hair looks like a flame, curling wildly and flung in every direction.

I fucked her into exhaustion last night, and there's no one to chastise me for the pride I feel about that. Careful and quiet, I grab my sword and knives. She hasn't showed any sign of waking. I might as well train if I'm going to be on guard anyway.

But I can't stop myself from leaning down and pressing a kiss to her temple, feeling the bond solidify with our proximity. She smells like sweetness and sex—the perfect combination. I whisper the words "I love you," into her hair. She doesn't stir, but she doesn't have to. She'll understand the words anyway.

CHAPTER SEVEN

KARI

I can tell that it's well past midday when I wake up. The same way that I've woken up the last three days, because my newly sealed mate is determined to pleasure me into absolute exhaustion.

My body feels like it's run a marathon, and in a way it has. Aeric took me in every way possible last night. Every night since we sealed that bond. The tantalizing magic and the newness of being able to *feel* driving us back into each other's arms more than I expected we could. Until the bright begins to touch the sky, the candles that Aeric prefers burning low in pools of shimmering wax, and we fall asleep tangled in each other.

Now, though, I find myself alone in Aeric's bed. I'm completely naked, and the cuffs he used to bind me to the four posts of his bed are gone from my wrists and ankles, though I fell asleep with them on.

Goddess, I feel like I could sleep for a week. It's that exquisite exhaustion that comes from too much sex. If there is such a thing. Slowly, I stretch, feeling the soreness and tight spots. But I honestly don't want to get out of this bed.

To their unending credit, not one of the other guys has complained about the amount of time I've spent in Aeric's bed. In fact, I've seen them almost laughing about it. Sharing amused looks whenever Aeric hauls me into his lap during a meal or when he carried me like a caveman to this room last night. The fact that they manage to handle whatever jealousy they might have is still a miracle to me. I'm not sure that I would handle the same situation as well.

Plus, they'll all get their turn.

One good thing about this is that I've been distracted from Ariana. Part of it, I know is intentional. Every time I start to worry, or they leave to go scout for traces of Ariana's magic, or they share a look that makes me wonder if they're hiding something, I end up glowing with magic and being driven mad by Aeric's ferocious intensity.

But just like it has when I start to think about it, the frustration comes back. I'm sick of waiting. I need to act, and every day that goes by makes the itch under my skin worse. I don't know if that's coming from my lack of power, our lack of knowledge, or if I'm being pushed to fucking *do* something.

So far there's been no sign of Ariana, but she's there in the back of my mind. Why did she want to wait? She never does anything without a reason. That friction and frustration is building in me. As much as I love the sex and the pleasure, I *hate* just waiting.

Something has to give. Which might be part of her plan too. Driving me crazy so that by the time the meeting comes around I'm more pliable. I definitely wouldn't put it past her. I put nothing past her.

The door opens, and Aeric slips in, fully dressed. He has a glass of water and a plate of food. And what looks like a robe draped over his arm. He smiles. "I felt you wake up."

"I might be going back to sleep."

His smirk deepens as he passes me the glass of water. "I would consider it a victory if you did, but you can't."

The water is so good. Fuck, I didn't realize how thirsty I was. Marathon sex requires hydration. "Why to both of those statements?"

Aeric puts the plate—which I can see now is fruit and waffles—on the bedside table and stretches out beside me. His hand lands naturally on the curve of my waist, and I love this. The connection has pulled us closer and is allowing us to be…easy. Natural in a way that we hadn't yet achieved.

"First," Aeric says. "Knowing that I fucked my

mate hard enough that she can't get out of bed would be a point of pride. And second, you can't go back to sleep because you have a visitor. I mean you could, but I think that might be rude."

"A visitor?" I can't imagine who could possibly be visiting me, except for people we don't *want* to visit. "Am I going to *like* this visitor?"

He smirks. "I think so."

"Okay." I push myself into a sitting position, holding steady for a moment. "I need to take a bath. And maybe some clothes since you keep shredding my underwear." Just like I thought I might have to, I need to send a message to Kaya about more.

Aeric stands and holds up the robe—one of my favorites. "I did warn you about the underwear, and I honestly don't think that she'll care that much if you have a bath."

My eyebrows rise into my hair. "She?"

He smiles again as he helps me into the sleeves. "Yes. Kent and Brae went to New York this morning to check on Emma and Odette. As far as Brae can tell, Ariana or anyone connected to her hasn't been there since the fire. Nothing remotely close to your friends." He presses a gentle kiss to my lips. "You've been anxious, and they thought you might feel better if you talked to someone who wasn't the five of us."

My whole mood brightens. "Emma is here?"

Aeric nods, smiling.

I move too quickly and I stumble before catching myself. Goddess, I really didn't know that it was possible to have trouble walking after sex, but these past few days have proven that it's very possible. I feel like my legs might give out. And I intentionally ignore Aeric's chuckle behind me, because he notices. I can feel the primal male satisfaction streaming through our bond, and I send back the emotional equivalent of the middle finger.

That only makes him laugh harder.

Heading down the stairs, my entire mood lifts. I'm not sure which of the guys thought I needed a friend—or if it was all of them—but the thought of just relaxing and talking someone is relieving. I turn the corner into the living room, and Emma is sitting on one of the couches across from Kent and Brae. Her face lights up when she sees me. "Hi."

I'm across the space to her in seconds, reaching out and pulling Emma into a hug that she returns even harder. We've always had hug competitions—who can nearly crush the other. Today she almost wins. "I'm so happy to see you," I say, but the truth is laced with anxiety, and I look back at the men. "But is it safe that she's here?"

Brae nods. "We took precautions, and warded Emma's apartment as solidly as the mansion. We're not hiding now. They know where we are. But there was nothing within a mile of her."

"Okay." I won't lie, having her here is perfect. I little tightness in my chest that I'd never noticed eases. "Who's idea was it?" I ask them.

"All of us," Brae says immediately. It's a lie that I let slide.

I look back over at my friend. "Should I give you the grand tour?"

Emma grins. "Hell yes. Given that this room is like three times the size of my actual apartment."

Kent gestures. "We'll give you two some time to catch up." He and Brae quietly disappear, leaving the two of us alone, and as soon as they're gone I hug Emma again.

"It really is good to see you."

"You too! Though I think I maybe could have come at a better time."

"Why?"

She gives me a look. "Have you looked in a mirror, Kari? I'm not sure there's ever been a clearer example of 'freshly fucked' than you right now."

I roll my eyes. "I told Aeric I wanted to bathe first and he convinced me not to."

"I don't care, but girl you must have gotten it *good* last night." She laughs when I blush all the way to my hairline. "I'm going to need you to tell me everything though."

"Emma."

"Kari," she responds, eyes lit up with amusement. "Odette wanted to come, by the way. But she's in the middle of full-length rehearsals for *Swan Lake*."

"Damn," I say. Those are some of the most intense rehearsals. That role is difficult and demanding, and as sure as I am that Odette will absolutely be *amazing*, I'm not surprised that she doesn't have the time to spare. "Give her my love."

"Of course." Emma loops her arm through mine as I lead her towards the stairs. I give her a quick overview of the house. The baths and the gardens, kitchen and libraries—yes, more than one—and probably a dozen rooms or more that I haven't even explored. Given the way the house rearranges at will, I can never really be sure if I've seen it all. "Wait," Emma says. "You mean the house is sentient?"

I laugh. "Kind of, yeah."

"That is so fucking cool." It's a whisper under her breath but I still hear it.

Up the stairs I point around the balcony. "Everyone's rooms."

Emma shakes her head in disbelief. "I know that it's not crazy, but it's also a little crazy, you know?"

"Welcome to my every day thought process," I say as I lead her into my room.

She stops. "Holy shit."

"I know," I say. "Speaking of being freshly fucked do you care if I get in the bath?"

Emma laughs and shakes her head. "Lord knows we've seen each other naked enough times."

That's true. When you're in the corps together, everything from dressing rooms to costume changes, there's not a lot of room or time for modesty. After a while everyone is so close that you just don't think about it. "Thanks." I quickly toss the robe aside and sink into my pool with the fountains, loving the warmth of it.

The magic-infused water lets off eddies of light, trailing behind my movement. I can't help but notice that today those little glowing fragments are the pale green that I always imagine Aeric's magic to be. Like hell am I going to tell him that though. If he knew that he'd fucked so much magic into me that I was literally leaking it, I'd never hear the end of it for the rest of our lives.

I shouldn't be surprised though. There have been several points in the last few days where I've been glowing with power, and I think he was a little bit too. I didn't even think about how much magic we've been generating, but I'm guessing that the whole fucking house feels it. That used to bother me.

It doesn't anymore.

"So," Emma says, huge grin on her face. "Start with last night and then fill me in on everything that's happened since you disappeared into something that looked like the Matrix."

She's talking about when the shop burned. I still try not to think about it. Even though I'm fine with it, it's probably going to be a long time before I don't have an ache in my chest when I think about it. That was something I built from scratch, and it'll always be precious to me for that reason. Thankfully, I have what I need. I can see the bottles of herbs and oils that I rescued before it burned. They're on a gorgeously carved shelf that appeared one day, everything already catalogued the way I would have done it. Because the mansion is that good.

"Well, three days ago—" I clear my throat and grab a bottle of shampoo from the side of the tub. "Aeric and I mated."

Emma frowns. "I thought you were already mates?"

"We were. Are. But there's a way to seal that bond and make it real. You have to choose it. And *no*, I'm not going to tell you how," I say as soon as she opens her mouth to ask it.

She pouts. "You're no fun."

I make a face, but in a way she's right. Nothing I'm doing with any of the guys is wrong. And even though I don't plan on being an open sexual book to everyone, my friends can know. I need to let go of this shame and embarrassment whenever I talk about us. Especially about something that was actually incredibly beautiful. "Fine."

Emma has about the same reaction that I did when I heard about the ritual. She's laughing so hard that she almost falls off my bed, and I admit that it is hilarious. But at the same time, now that I'm on the other side of it I understand why the fae treated it with such reverence. "You're not laughing," she says.

"I did. When I first heard. But now…I honestly don't know how to explain it, Emma. I can *feel* him right here." I touch my chest below my heart. "It's going to sound bitchy and condescending but I don't think it's something that anyone could understand unless you've felt it."

"No," she shakes her head. "You're right. I'm sorry for laughing."

I snort. "Don't be. When I heard I could barely keep my shit together. But I guess it's not the same in every court, but the main common denominator is that it's a selfless act between the two people."

"And you need to do this…four more times?"

Before I answer, I duck under the water and rinse the soap from my hair. "I wish that were an easier question," I say while I swipe the water from my eyes.

Emma smirks, stretching out on the bed and doing the ballet repetitions that we all used to do in the corps—probably without even realizing she's doing it. That's how deeply those were drilled into us. "Which part tripped you up."

"Well," I say, wringing the water from my hair and grabbing a sponge to quickly wash the rest of me. "Kent isn't Fae. So I don't know if there's a way to create the same bond with him. And turns out I have one more Fae mate, who tried to kill me and is under the influence of the evil bitch who's after me."

"I'm sorry, *what?*"

"Yeah," I laugh. "Tell me about it. This would be the part where I fill you in on the rest of it."

I dry myself off and dress while I tell her all of it. When she tells all of this to Odette—and she will—I can't even imagine the commentary that she's going to add. When I finish, she's quiet. "Now I get why you were asking if it's safe for me to be here."

That creeping anxiety coils across my limbs like a snake—I can't help it. I don't even know what to say to that, because I'm wondering that too. But as long as she's here, and at home, she'll be safe. And Ariana has no reason to go after Emma if I show up at that rendezvous, and I'm going to be there.

"It seemed like it when you were in New York, but I didn't really get the chance to ask. Even with everything that's happening…are you happy?"

I sit down beside her on the bed and lean my shoulder on hers. "Yeah, I am. It's nothing that I ever would have thought I wanted. And ninety-eight percent of the fucking time it all feels impossible. But I love them."

"I guess that's worth missing you, then." She's trying to hide the emotion in her voice, but she can't.

I hug her as best as I can the way I'm beside her, and she hugs me back. "I'm not dead."

She laughs. "I know, but it's not going to be the same."

"If you think that after this is all over I'm not coming to New York to bug your ass, see your shows, and get some decent fucking pizza, you're crazy."

Emma laughs, falling back on the bed. "Are you serious? They don't have pizza here?"

"I'm sure the house would make me some, but I haven't seen any pizza joints in the markets around here."

She smirks. "Guess Allwyn doesn't have everything."

"Not everything. Do you have rehearsal today?"

"Day off today. Full run of *Giselle* tomorrow though."

I wince. "Ugh. Make sure to stretch your feet tonight *and* in the morning."

"I'm planning on it." Emma is playing Myrtha, queen of the maiden spirits. It's not an easy role either. "Is there some kind of jacked up time shit between earth and Allwyn that I have to worry about so that I need to leave before I'm gone for a week?"

"Not that I know of, thankfully. That would get old fucking fast."

She hops off the bed, practically bouncing. "Good. Makes scheduling easier too. I want to come back as soon as I can."

I give her a look. "There's an invisible 'but' in that sentence."

Wandering over to my bookshelf, she runs her fingers over a picture frame sitting on it. It's of her, Odette, and I, back when we were all baby ballerinas in the corps. We're dressed in flowing Arabian costumes from *Le Corsaire*. Probably one of my least favorite ballets, but with them it was always fun. "But, I need to go because I have a date tonight."

"Okay, wait," I say standing. "You should have led with that! Who? Please tell me it's not Peter. I know he's hot, but that man is not worth it, Emma." Peter is one of the principals in the ballet company, and Emma had a crush on him for years. He's hot as sin, but also an idiot and kind of a pig.

She smiles, but it's in a soft way that I've never seen before. "It's not Peter. It's not anyone from the company, actually."

I gasp in mock drama. "You dare to date *outside* the ballet world?! How *dare* you."

"You can laugh but there were a couple of girls who reacted that way."

"I don't doubt it." Ballet people can be picky about almost everything, including thinking that no one outside of the world of dance could possibly understand the demands of being a dancer. But I never bought into it, and the few relationships I had while I was still dancing were always with people who were as far from dancers as you could get. "I'm happy for you. First date?"

She shakes her head. "No. Third date."

"Oh my god, woman. You're telling me you have to get ready to go have sex and I'm keeping you here?" I playfully grab her arm and pull her down the stairs while she laughs. "The way you pressure me for details about my sex life, I can't believe you didn't tell me."

"I know," Emma says. "But he's different. And I'm not sure where it's going yet."

I look her straight in the eyes. "If he hurts you, I'll kill him. So will Odette. Make sure he knows that."

Emma makes a face. "I'm not so sure that it will come up."

"I could send one of the guys to make sure the point hits home," I say, pulling her into a hug.

She makes her face but her eyes are laughing. "Please don't. I don't need your tall, devastatingly handsome men intimidating my date."

"Oh fine. But will you tell me how it goes?"

"How?"

I shrug. "I'm learning magic. I'll have one of the guys teach me to create a magical phone call. Or a magical wifi network."

"Sounds good." Emma hugs me again. "I really do miss you," she says softly. "Please be careful."

"We're always careful," Aeric says from behind me.

Emma shakes her head and rolls her eyes, and I give him a look. "I told you guys that that sentiment isn't comforting."

His amusement plays through the bond like a trickle of playful warmth. "I know." He focuses on Emma. "Will you allow me to transport you home?"

"Of course."

We hug one more time, giving in to our hug competition before she waves goodbye. I don't miss the glassy eyes that she tries to hide. She's a badass, and strong, but I think she's lonely right now. With me here in Allwyn and Odette rehearsing straight through the day, I can imagine she feels a little isolated. I'm glad she has a date, and that it was safe enough to bring her here. It was something that we both needed.

I walk back toward my bedroom, and walk into the courtyard to find Kent, Verys, and Urien talking. But they stop when I walk in. Kent smiles. "Emma leave?"

That's not his real smile.

"Yeah. What's going on?" Over the last few days I've noticed this. They've been cagey and are working together to make sure I don't ask the questions that are about to burst.

"Nothing," Verys says quickly. "Just filling Urien in on New York."

I look at them each in turn. It's clearly not that, and they're clearly acting weird. Kent sighs and looks at them. "We agreed to tell her."

Immediately I'm on guard. "Tell me what?"

Behind me, Brae's voice is quiet. "About the deliveries."

CHAPTER EIGHT

KARI

"Show me."

Brae shakes his head. "Everything is gone. We destroyed it in case there were any curses or invasive magic attached. And trust me when I say that you wouldn't want to see."

I feel sick. Anger like poison spreading with every heartbeat. Over the last few weeks, I've tried to put myself in Ariana's shoes, if only for a moment so that I could try to understand where she might be coming from. What possible reason that she could have for attacking and fixating on me—and now my mates.

But I've got fucking nothing. Who *does* this? I can't comprehend the kind of person that sends messages of death, and beyond that, the careless way she treats others and their lives. Five fae have been damaged permanently by her ambition—whatever that is—and from what I've seen with Kiaran those fae might not even be in their right mind.

"Can we send a message?" I ask. "Tell her we plan on meeting her so that she'll stop?"

"Where would we send it?" Kent asks. "And I don't like the idea of us admitting to anything beforehand. It puts us in a bad position."

"We're already in a bad position," I snap. "And I don't want bodies to be the next thing that show up on our doorstep. Ariana is a psychopath, and I know I'm not responsible for her actions, but I don't want blood on my hands because there was something easy that we just didn't try."

"You really think sending her a message will get her to stop?" Kent asks. "There's a reason not negotiating is the hard line that a lot of people stick to. You give them anything and they see that they're getting to you, they'll come at you that much harder."

I reach down into that well of magic that's inside me and bring it up and out. My magic is so much stronger than I'm used to. Probably because I've been gathering power like crazy in my time with Aeric. Inside it feels like a torrent of blue and gold flame.

With the power gathering in me I feel a sense of ease and purpose that I haven't felt in forever. This, I can do something with. The Goddess's magic sings under my skin, sparkles like a never-ending river, encouraging me to push and move and make.

I don't question it. I turn away from the guys, and go out of the house into the gardens. My feet are leading themselves, or maybe the goddess is leading me. I end up in the labyrinth. The stone carving that marks the center of the land.

Everything in the gardens seems to shimmer. Details draw my eyes in flashes, each one more beautiful than the last. Turquoise trees shivering against the crimson sky. Intricately carved stone beneath my feet, shining with pale light. Rainbows glinting through the water of the fountains and waterfalls. Clusters of flowers I've never noticed, and couldn't name because they're not in the human realm. Some look a little like daisies and some of them look like stars. I swear that everything is shining.

Not enough.

The whisper is soft but clear. I'm not holding enough magic. I close my eyes and reach for my own, that twisting thread of violet fire, and I wrap it around my soul. Then I take a deep breath and plunge into the fountain of the goddess's magic with both hands.

A rush of light and power so complete washes over me. I am the magic, and it is me. It fuses to my bones and binds itself around my veins and suddenly I think that I can hear the universe. There are voices —maybe shouting—and in my body. I can sense emotions like awe and fear, but they don't feel like mine.

Around me I can feel the life in the air, the plants, and the five bright sparks of life more vibrant than the rest. I can sense the wards, swirling and stretching around us, and I know that I can make them stronger. Another shield just like mine—spun from golden glass, woven and webbed with fluid energy. Nothing can walk past this shield without my consent, or that of the Goddess. Even coming near it could be fatal.

It's like a wall charged with a million volts of current, hovering just beneath the visible surface of things. Anyone who dares to come close will feel the power.

The scent of roses is thick in the air, as is the feeling of perfect security. No one can touch us. Anyone. Especially not her.

"Show me," I whisper. I'm asking the Goddess. Her power. My power. Take me to her.

The space in front of me transforms, and I'm in darkness with Ariana. She's an apparition—there and not there all at once. The only light for her is the speck of orange power hovering above her fingertips, and now, me.

There are rocks smooth and shiny as glass, but twisted. Molten like they've been melted and reformed. She turns when I appear, momentary shock quickly covered up by her usual arch smile. "Kari."

"End this," I say. "Tomorrow."

She purses her lips, pretending to consider. But we both know she's already chosen to agree. "So eager to embrace your fate?" She asks.

"Eager to stop you from harming anymore fae in order to send a message."

Ariana's eyes sparkle, and she laughs like she's just been given the best gift of her life. "Did you enjoy the presents?"

I don't answer.

"I suppose I can move up our meeting. Things are almost ready to begin." She takes a step towards me, and beneath this shell of power I'm holding onto, my body shrinks in terror. She's not here and I'm not there, and yet my mind recoils when she reaches out and brushes her fingers down my cheek. It's nothing but a brush of air, and yet it's still revolting.

"Tomorrow," I say again, and I release that vision. She's gone, and I'm in the garden again. Visceral relief drops through me like a stone. This was the right decision. Even if it wasn't, it's done now.

Magic is still burning in my limbs—more than I've ever held before—and I try to let it go. And that's when the magic turns.

Power like this doesn't like to be contained, and I'm not its real master. I opened a door I don't know how to close—just a vessel for this power that's now trying to consume me in order to be free. First it was not enough, and now it's too much.

Panic wraps around my neck like a snake. I can barely breathe, the glory of power burning through me faster than I can manage to control it. It doesn't hurt. There's too much of it for that. It shines too much and soothes as it consumes. I need to release it. Get it out.

Throwing my hands outward I pour magic into the air, willing it to find a place that is not me. Create something new. But the gate I pushed through is still open, and I can't pull it back. New magic pours in and fills up the space. I'm a conduit and nothing more.

Help. I send the word outward towards that place where the Goddess's whispers live. *Help me.*

Skin collides with mine. One arm wrapped around my waist and another cradling my face. There's a voice in my ear. "Find your own magic Kari. Find it."

That means going deeper into the storm of power, and that will destroy what I have left. I feel like I'm unraveling. What happens when you get consumed by magic? Do you die or do you become a part of that magic too? Death like this might be less painful. I shake my head.

"Find it."

The words clear my mind for a moment of the golden, glittery haze. There. A flash of the violet. I reach for it and manage to hold it. Spin it around my hands and keep it close. It's barely anything in comparison to that storm, but suddenly I can breathe again because holding my magic makes me let go of all the rest of it.

I hadn't even realized that I was gathering it to myself and keeping it there. The core of power collapses in on itself, back to the glowing, infinite ember. My knees buckle, but I'm held upright. The rest of the power is still sizzling under my skin with nowhere to go—far too much for a human. It's pouring out of me and into him, but it's still not enough of a diversion to save me.

"Make something," the voice says. "Anything."

I don't even think, or it feels like I don't. There's a cracking sound like thunder, and shaking. I manage to open my eyes to see the tree. It was the first thing that popped into my head. A giant, weeping tree in full bloom. The colors of the blossoms come from every corner of the spectrum, and the branches bow to create a curtain around us. Brae and I.

It's Brae holding me. Grounding me.

Beneath our feet the stone of the labyrinth is cracked and broken to make way for the trunk of the tree, and it's still growing. As it does, the storming power in me subsides, channeling into the plant.

I sag into Brae's arms when it's gone. I'm whole, but I might not have been, if he hadn't helped. And the most frightening thing is that I wasn't afraid. Yet another moment where I had to choose, though I wasn't prompted. It could have been easy to fade into the magic and completely let go. I'm still hazy now, the aftermath of it swimming behind my eyes.

Brae pulled me back, thank the Goddess. No matter what happens, I am not finished yet. Not with this life and not with these men.

His power warms me like the feeling of the sun on your face after weeks of winter. It doesn't consume, it seeks. Testing me and seeing if I'm whole and unharmed. Gently, he helps me to sit and rest against the base of this new, god-touched tree. And now I'm having deja vu, because this position is so similar to our very first encounter. In that cave. Where his fingers and the promise of pleasure kept me alive.

"Brae," I pull him to me, yanking his face to mine to kiss him.

He falls into it with me, messy and raw and desperate. "I thought I had made peace with the danger," he says, lips barely leaving mine. "But every time I almost lose you, I learn that I'm wrong."

Brae's eyes are green, but they're such a different green than Aeric's. They're deep and dark, and right now rich with emotion and pain. "You're not going to lose me."

His hand comes up to cup my face again, along with his desperate kiss. "You can't know that. But I'm going to fight like hell for you, even if I have to let you pour an entire world's worth of magic into me."

The gentle touch of his lips and one stroke of his magic bring me to clarity, and it's like stepping out from under cloud cover. I could have died. Would have died. "I couldn't stop it," I whisper. "I'm so sorry." My throat is thick with emotion.

Brae pulls me close, wrapping his arms around me.

"Don't let me go."

He knows that I don't mean with his arms.

He is *mine*, and he's still too far away from me. I need more of it and more of him. I need everything. I can't feel him, and that is unfathomable to me. The bond between us is almost singing and it hasn't even formed yet. "Do you feel it?"

"Yes," his voice is rough.

My hands are shaking, still weak, but I reach for

him, fumbling with his trousers. He's already hard under my hands, and I am more than ready for this. I know what's coming now, and I intend to savor every moment and sensation.

Even standing, Brae keeps his hand on my cheek, runs his fingers through my hair. Those tendrils of connection forming between us tell me that he wishes we could be face to face for this. There will be time for that. I plan on having a lot of face-to-face time with him.

The look of love on his face nearly knocks me back. My chest surges with pure emotion, and our magic entwines together before heaven touches my lips.

Brae tastes like light. If that were a flavor. Brightness and shine and sweetness. Buttery yellow candy and hot summer days. A moan escapes me, and I suck him in deeper.

He's thick, and long, curving upward, tan and nearly golden like the rest of his gorgeous skin. There's none of the nervousness that I felt with Aeric. I know what's coming next, and I can't wait.

"Goddess, Kari," Brae murmurs. Awe and adoration color his tone. I feel it too. I love the feel of him in my mouth and sliding against my tongue, but this is a whole new experience with him. Of course it's about pleasure—selfless and pure—but it's also about needing that bond with him the way I've never needed anything before.

I crave that closeness and that knowledge. I crave the taste of him and his magic. I crave being able to tell exactly what he wants and makes him feel good.

Every muscle in Brae's body is tight and coiled. He's braced against the tree above me, lips parted and eyes closed. I use my tongue, swirling it over the head of his cock and diving onto him before doing it again. His breath hitches, and I feel the swell of our magic together.

For a moment, I focus on just the tip of him. Using my lips to seal my mouth around him create that suction that makes him groan. "Fuck."

Brae's hips move, thrusting forward even though it feels like he's desperately trying to hold back. If he wants more, I'll give him more. Hell, so do I. When he pushes forward I take him in, nearly swallowing. Letting him fill my mouth all the way.

He curses, using words and slang that I've never heard before when I release him to take a breath. And then I take him again. This time I don't stop, rising up to angle him into my throat. The sensation of him entering me so deeply sends arousal and need and power through me.

I hold myself on his cock as long as I can, working him with my throat, gripping his hips to keep him close. Dragging my tongue along his shaft, I catch my breath for a moment. But when I reach the tip and tease his underside—tasting the magic already leaking from his cock—I know.

Now.

Seal the bond now.

I look up at Brae as I suck him fast and hard into my mouth, tightening my lips so all he can feel is me and the rhythm I set. Fast and not stopping, not until he spills everything he has on my tongue.

Our magic spirals towards each other as if pulled by gravity. Spinning and twisting and melding together as one. Brae opens his eyes, and he doesn't have to speak. I know. He's there.

Power explodes between us as he finishes, yelling his climax into the trees. Pure bright light. Gilded sweetness like tasting pure gold. I swallow it entirely, feeling the power seep into me and suddenly those bits of our magic that are spinning together merge. Into something new. Irrevocably changed.

A little piece of my magic disappears into him at the same time that the bright spot of his settles in my chest. Right next to where Aeric's magic lies, but so wholly different there's no mistaking it.

Brae pulls away, sinking to his knees in front of me. It's like containing a bit of sunlight directly in my soul, and I ache with it. With the need to have him closer.

He doesn't need me to ask now—not when he can sense it. Our positions are reversed in seconds, with me straddling his lap while he reclines against the tree. Arms hold me close. But I'm holding him back just as hard.

What I'm feeling from him is…everything. Shock and wonderment and gratitude. "I didn't—" He cuts off. "I didn't know it would be like this."

"Good?"

He pulls my face up from where it's pressed into his neck. "Amazing." And then he's kissing me. Just as desperately as before. More so, now that he can feel exactly what it's doing to me.

Sunny magic leaks from his mouth into mine, enhancing the flavor of him still on my tongue.

"I didn't plan that," I say. "Obviously. I just knew that I needed you. Needed this."

He smiles softly. "You can't plan for things like this. I felt it too."

It makes me wonder what the other bondings will be like. Sealing my bond with Aeric was about showing him the love that I feel for him—showing him his value and allowing him to realize how much I love him. Between Brae and I it spun itself for us, knitting us together in a way we didn't plan and didn't prepare for. Neither is better or less valid. Just different. I imagine the others will be similarly unique.

Glancing around, I examine the curtain of flowers shielding us from the rest of the gardens. But not just flowers. Roses. New plants with as many varieties of the flower as are in that place in the market to get offerings. Copper and gold, violet, turquoise, gorgeous ombre and swirling ripples in hue. This came out of me. Out of the magic I was given. It's beautiful. And terrifying.

I tuck my head down onto his shoulder again. "Why did that happen? Why couldn't I stop?"

He pushes down the immediate worry that surfaces. "You're still new to the use of big magic, Kari. And I'm not sure you realize exactly how big it is, what you did."

"I made a shield. I talked to Ariana. I made a tree. Yeah, that's a lot, but I wouldn't think it's out of the realm of possibility for Allwyn or Cerys."

Fingers trace down my spine, and I arch into him, enjoying the goosebumps. "You didn't just make a shield. You made an *impenetrable* shield. I've never felt anything like it. Nothing is getting through that. Hell, we're probably going to get questions from the neighbors. I'd be surprised if the entire Court didn't feel the magic that was coming off you. You were glowing just like when I found you at the temple."

He shakes his head, "And I have no idea where Ariana is, but you projected yourself to her. And she's not close. That takes power. A lot of it. You're not used to holding that much, especially when it's not yours. Maybe with practice, but it would need to be careful practice."

"Yeah," I say. "It didn't hurt. I could feel that I was panicking, but that was secondary. You brought me back."

"I always will." He kisses me softly again. "Always."

Leaning into the kiss, I run my hands over his shoulders and feel the way his body is reacting beneath mine. *Yes.*

I gasp, jumping off his lap, reacting to the stinging sensation before I can see what it is. Then it happens again, like a splatter of fiery pin-pricks into my skin.

Brae is on his feet instantly. "Kari?"

"What is that?" It happens a third time.

He places his palm on my cheek and closes his eyes. I wince when the next barrage hits, and Brae nods. "She's testing the shield."

"That's the shield?"

"Wards that use your power are connected to

you, so you can feel if anything happens. It's how we knew that Kiaran was here so quickly."

Another, stronger sensation. Like someone has thrown a bucket of acid into the shield. I hiss, because it hurts. And yet it doesn't. It's all in my mind. "That's annoying."

"This you will get better at quickly. New wards are more sensitive, and you'll be able to tune out anything accidental or not important."

"Hopefully we won't need it for too long anyway," I mutter. "I told Ariana we would meet her tomorrow."

I can feel his surprise so strongly through the new bond, it resonates in my chest. "Really?"

"Yes."

He nods. "All right. We'll make sure that we're ready. Let's get you back to the house before you collapse from exhaustion."

"You think?"

The laugh that rings out through the gardens is loud and joyful, and my whole body lights up with the sound. "With that amount of magic, I'll be surprised if you wake up in time to make the meeting tomorrow."

I pout as he pulls me into the house. "But that means skipping our mating night."

Brae looks at me, dark eyes even darker with

promise. "We won't be skipping anything. Every night for the rest of our lives can be mating night."

"I like the sound of that."

A weight like an anvil crashes down on top of the shield, and I lose my breath for a moment. "That's going to be annoying."

"If all she does between now and tomorrow is attack that shield, then I'll be grateful." But now Brae is looking towards the front door. "Someone's here."

Together, we walk into the entryway. Urien is speaking with a fae I don't know. She has some kind of uniform on. It's not a long conversation. Just a passage of a message from one to the other, and then she's gone. "Anything interesting?" Brae asks.

"Maybe," Urien says. A shimmer of light comes from the piece of paper he was given, and he scans it quickly. His face goes slack with shock.

"What is it?"

Urien clears his throat. "There was a disturbance at the Heart of Allwyn. An earthquake. Not native magic."

The dread I feel coming off Brae nearly makes me ill. "Really?"

"What does that mean?"

Urien's golden eyes focus on me. "The Heart of Allwyn is where Cerys is buried. A mountain where the remaking occurred. Her body is encased there. Preserved by her power."

Shit. That is bad.

"Kari," Brae says. "Where was Ariana when you saw her?"

I shake my head. "It was dark. The most I could see was some rock that looked like it had been melted and frozen. You think she's there?" That core of magic deep in my gut whispers *yes*, before either of them have the chance to speak.

"Likely," Urien says. "And if she is, what Kiaran said about her re-making the world carries more weight."

"Do you think she wants to resurrect Cerys?" Aeric asks, and I jump. I hadn't seen him in the living room, lounging on one of the couches.

"I'm not sure why she would want to do that," Brae says, shaking his head. "But if that's what she wants, it lines up with her stealing magic. And being fixated on Kari's."

A tiny bit of tension releases from my shoulders, like a puzzle piece has clicked. After so much not knowing what kind of motivation she has, anything is good. Even if it is as dire as this.

"Can you find out more?" I ask Urien.

"Yes. I'll go to the palace and ask. I'm guessing they didn't put too much detail in the message for good reason. I'll see if there's any information on Ariana I can find while I'm there. Without raising too many alarms."

Brae waves. "Use that Tiarne status for our benefit."

Urien shakes his head, but he's smiling as he leaves. Aeric isn't smiling. I can see the tension coming off him as much as I can feel it.

"Give us a minute, Brae."

He melts into the background without saying a word, and I wrap my arms around Aeric. It takes him a moment to respond, but when he does he holds me tight. His feelings are shifting quickly, and I gather them all. He's hurting and fighting the hurt. Trying to breathe through it and be okay, even though he's not. He respects Brae and *wants* to be okay with it, even if he isn't.

"I didn't plan it," I whisper. "It just...happened. I knew it needed to happen. I'm—"

"Don't apologize," he says quietly. "He's your mate."

"You are too."

He smiles, but I can still see the pain in his eyes. "Yes, I am. And I love you."

"Still?"

His kiss takes me by surprise. Ravenous and powerful. I melt against him, sinking into that control. He doesn't have to say the words. I feel them in my chest. *I love you. I love you. I love you.*

My knees are weak and shaking when he releases me, and not just from the kiss. Energy is pouring out of my body at an alarming rate, and Aeric catches me before I hit the floor. "I need to kiss you like that more often," he says.

"Smartass." I say, but there's no power behind the word. I'm entirely limp, and I don't like the feeling.

"Brae," Aeric calls, voice echoing through the hall.

There's a moment, when one man passes me to the other. A silent acknowledgement of what this means, and the significance. Aeric is perfectly capable of carrying me to bed—he's done it more than once in the past few days.

But he's choosing not to. Choosing to pass me to Brae, who's cradling me in his arms now. They nod to each other, and for the first time I feel a sense of calm from Aeric about the situation. Good.

But all I can do is send gratitude through the bond, because I'm already asleep.

CHAPTER NINE

KARI

This dream is different. I can feel that right away. It's not the murky darkness in which I usually meet Kiaran. This seems more real. Maybe it's because I'm in a deeper sleep from all that magic? Maybe it's just an aftermath of that.

I'm standing in a cavern made of crystal. Or that's what it seems like in the semi-darkness. There are facets of stone and molten flows of that same material. But this isn't the Crystal Court. I know that, deep in my core.

Where we are is familiar, and I could swear that I've stood in this exact spot. Except for the fact that I know I've never set foot in this place before.

Kari.

The whisper comes from beside me, and Kiaran steps up beside me. He doesn't look at me, and when I reach out to touch him, he's there. The fabric of his shirt is soft under my fingers, muscles hard underneath that. But he doesn't react to me. Is this a dream or a vision? Does he know I'm here?

He walks past me, and I follow him. Deeper into

the cavern where a pulse of power beats. A deep, thrumming vibration that I can feel in my bones, and that I recognize. It's a deeper version of the one that's inside me now. That golden, glittering mass that I was given is only a drop of this, but I would recognize that magic anywhere. That's Cerys's power.

Kiaran steps around a formation of rocks, and suddenly the space around us opens up into what feels like infinity. Spheres of magic hover in the air high above us, casting light around the space. Crystalline rocks shimmer in every hue, shattering prisms into rainbows across the gathered fae. At first glance there are maybe twenty, all of them with a dead expression and that manic gleam in their eyes that speaks of being controlled.

The cavern is roughly circular, and the floor flatter than I would have expected for something that looks so natural. But on that detail alone, I know that it's not. The ground is stone too, and clear. It's like looking down into water, the light fading at a certain distance leaving the impression of vast depth and unease. The thrumming is coming from somewhere in that depth, hidden, yet palpable.

And straight ahead of where Kiaran's walking, the ground appears to have erupted. Jagged, broken chunks of glassy stone shear straight up and out at odd angels. Debris litters the floor around it. Kiaran's steps crunch as he steps over the rubble. This was recent.

This was the earthquake. Not an accident or natural event. The beginning of an excavation.

Now I see where Kiaran is headed. Ariana is standing under one of the giant fragments, staring at the fae before her, their arms outstretched and caressing the stone with power. Little rocks crack off the surface onto the floor. They're digging through the chunk, one small bit of magic at a time.

Ariana turns and sees Kiaran, and she doesn't look happy. "This is going far slower than we thought it would."

Kiaran turns on a slow smile. "Are you really that surprised? This is the source of all magic in the world. It makes sense that it would protect itself."

"We're going to need more manpower."

"Once you have Kari's magic, it won't be a problem."

She rolls her eyes. "I can't use that magic for this. As powerful as she is, I don't know how much magic she has, and I need it for the final blow. I'm not going to waste that power getting to the vessel and not being able to finish the job. We need more fae."

I feel sick. She can't mean what I think she means. Can she?

"That can be arranged," Kiaran says, sticking his hands in his pockets. "It may start to draw attention."

"Start with the dark courts. There must be some fae who will come to us willingly. And if they won't, there are plenty there that won't be missed."

A loud *crack!* Rends the air, and a foot-sized chunk falls from one of the seams. Ariana waves a hand, and the rest of the fae who are not yet working on the stone lift their hands and lend their magic.

"How quickly—"

She cuts him off with a raised hand. "You said it yourself. We're going to draw attention. I need it fast enough to be completed. So as quickly as possible. So far things are falling in our favor. Are things ready for tomorrow?"

Kiaran nods. "All set."

"Keep hammering that stupid fucking shield. If anything it will grate on their nerves." She pauses, then smiles at him suddenly. Reaching out, she places a hand on his chest and runs it down across his abs. "The world will be ours, Kiaran. No one will be able to tell us who can and can't have magic. Where we belong. We'll belong everywhere."

He smiles down at her, but says nothing. I feel absolutely nauseated—can taste bile on my tongue. I don't want to see her touch him. Don't want to know what she forces him to do. He's very still, but for all the world with that smile on his face I would swear that he's in love with her.

"We still have time. Double check the holding and then go prepare the site."

Bowing his head, "As you wish."

When Kiaran turns, he looks directly at me. Not through me. Directly into my eyes, and they are clear. For this moment, he is his own person, and my breath rushes out of me all at once. He strides away and I follow him back into that smaller hallway, keeping as close as I dare to him.

The crackle of power is nearly a whisper when he changes direction, carrying me swiftly into the glassy wall and pinning me there. My gasp is lost in the kiss that sweeps me away, doubly stealing my breath. "You can touch me." It's more a statement than a question, and more a moan than anything else.

"Here it doesn't hurt."

His hands on me make me ache, that blue magic tasting and teasing and making me wish that this is more than a dream. "Did you bring me here? This isn't like the other dreams."

"You needed to see," he says. "Needed to know. And you had enough magic left for me to bring you here."

"What—"

"I'm sorry," he says. "I don't have time to explain it. I don't know how long I'll be clear. Only until she notices her charm has worn off. But you needed to see this. And be prepared for tomorrow. She's planning something."

Of course she is. I wouldn't expect her to do anything less. "What is it?"

"I don't know." When I raise my eyebrows he continues. "I swear on the Goddess that I don't know. You need to go now. Quickly." He starts to shake, fingers gripping my hips harder. Almost bruising. "I'll tell her, if you're here when I turn."

Panic grips my throat. "I don't know how to go back."

Kiaran kisses me hard, and I hold on to the moment for as long as I can. "Just open your eyes," he tells me. And then he's gone and I'm staring up into a different face.

Brae is hovering above me, face lit with worry and the magic pouring out of me. "Thank the Goddess," he breathes.

I shake my head a little to clear it. Blinking. What was that? Was it real? That nausea from the dream catches up with me, and I roll out of Brae's arms just in time to vomit over the side of my bed. Goddess bless magic, because within seconds the mess disappears, but the sick feeling in my stomach doesn't. I can't stop trying to throw up. She wants to kill her.

Ariana wants to kill the Goddess. That's what Kiaran meant when he said she wants to remake the world. Aeric was wrong. She doesn't want to resurrect her at all.

Hands smooth up my back, and I heave one more time, finally able to calm my stomach enough to stop. Brae's worry is leaking through the bond, even though he's doing his best to smother it with calm. "What happened?"

I shake my head, accepting the glass of water from him, and the help he offers to drink from it. It soothes my throat, but I can't seem to find my voice. Can't wrap my head around the fact that Ariana wants my magic to commit murder. It's so much bigger than I ever imagined.

Brae pulls me onto my back again, pulling me into his side. It's dark outside in the garden—probably some time in the middle of fade.

"You were glowing again," he says. "I couldn't wake you up."

I'm sure that he feels my panic and my dread, but I can't seem to reign it in. How do I tell him this? It's horrifying. I just shake my head—I don't want it to be true. *Please*.

Covering my face with my hands, I fight the

sheer, overwhelming terror that's binding itself to me. I never imagined this. Anything but this, actually. I thought it might be some kind of strange fixation since I was the one who got away. Maybe some good old-fashioned power trip. Use the power she wants to steal from me to take over a Kingdom or a Court. But this? The scope is too vast, and there's too much at stake. I can't be responsible for saving all of Allwyn.

Right?

That can't possibly be why I was given this power or why Allwyn chose me to be mated with Fae. Why me of everyone in the world? I can't make sense of it and my thoughts are spinning so fast that I can't slow them down.

"Kari," Brae says, pulling my hands away from my face. "Look at me. Breathe."

I try, but the air in my lungs is shaky at best.

"Tell me what happened."

I can't. There aren't words in my vocabulary for this. Something changes in his expression, and he rolls over me, sliding down my body with determined grace. He must have changed me into a nightgown after I passed out, because that's what I'm wearing, and it lets him push apart my legs with ease. His mouth lands on my clit without any prelude, grazing it with his teeth and rolling his tongue across it.

Holy shit.

Lust and pleasure blaze to life within me, the extreme height of my panic and dread morphing into bright, shining need. Brae was good at this before we bonded. Now, he's exquisite, listening to me and responding to what I like. That sweep of his tongue that makes my hips rise towards his lips and the way his fingers squeeze my inner thighs. He traces his tongue along the entrance to my pussy, and I moan—the first sound I've been able to make. I love that feeling. It's so intimate, and when he licks inside me I gush wetness onto his tongue.

Sunny magic slides up my skin, swirling across my nipples and pooling on them until they're diamond peaks, straining against the silk on my chest.

Brae moves his mouth upwards again, consuming my clit. He's not teasing me now, instead driving me straight to the edge, and over the edge. He pulls deeply, sucking me between his lips and squeezing, and I shatter. Pleasure washes up and over, magic breaking over the two of us together. He's just as turned on as I am by my orgasm, loving the feel of me.

He doesn't hesitate when he strips off his pants

and sinks deep into me. One smooth movement has him buried, and I'm staring up into his eyes, trying to breathe. That orgasm did exactly what he wanted it to—it broke the spiral of panic in my head and let me focus on him. And I am focusing on him. This is the first time he's been inside me with the bond, and I'm breathless at the feeling of fullness he brings me. His pleasure echoes mine. Heightens it.

His eyes are sharp, watching my expression closely. And when he thrusts the look on his face turns to both satisfaction and lust, because even the smallest movement makes me gasp, sensitive as I am after the pleasure of his mouth.

"What happened?"

"You want to know that now?" I ask, squeezing down on his cock. "I think it could wait a few minutes."

He thrusts again, intentionally dragging himself over my clit and making me shudder. He even adds a feathering of his magic, drawing goosebumps on the surface of my skin. "I just watched you glow with power and unable to wake up, and I've never felt anything like that panic. I'm more than satisfied being inside you, Kari. I'll wait. I'm patient."

"I don't know how to tell you," I say. "I don't even know what it was."

Brae rotates his hips slowly so his cock hits

different places inside of me. Then leaning down, he kisses me slowly. "As long as you keep talking, I'll keep moving. Otherwise nothing."

"Fuck you," I breathe, squeezing down on him in revenge, but there's no anger behind my words. I just want more of him and delicious, perfect ecstasy.

He grins. "I am trying. Talk."

"It wasn't a dream," I tell him. "More of a projection, like what I did with Ariana today, only one person could see me. I saw the Heart of Allwyn."

With deliberate slowness, Brae drives into me, slightly changing his angle with every movement, until suddenly he hits a place that makes my vision go white and my voice suddenly feel thin as mist. "What did you see?"

I think the best way is to just blurt it out. "Ariana is trying to dig up the Goddess's body. The earthquake was the beginning of the excavation. And she doesn't want to resurrect Cerys, she wants to kill her. I heard her say as much."

"To Kiaran?" He fucks a little harder, the sparks he's shoving into me catching on each other and building higher. I'm not surprised that he put two and two together, given what they know about my captured mate.

"Yes. She needs my magic—the Goddess's magic—for the final blow. That's all there was, and Kiaran said to make sure that we're ready for the meeting. That she's planning something."

Faster. Harder against that spot that makes me see nothing and feels so good that I'd be willing to go blind. "Why are you panicking?"

"It's too big," I say. "Too much. This can't be what's really happening. Because then that would mean that I'm in charge of the fate of Allwyn, and that's way more than—*oh!*" I lose my words again as Brae starts to fuck in earnest, rolling his hips so the motion hits every delicious spot. I'm so close again, hanging on the edge of bliss. Sinking into it.

"Please," I beg him. "More."

Tendrils of magic drag along my inner thighs, and that shivering touch sends me falling into bright oblivion over again. I cry out, voice echoing off the walls of my bedroom. But it's not over, because Brae isn't finished. I feel when he slips into me at the perfect angle and his pleasure soars. Just feeling that sharp slice of pleasure through our connection sets off aftershocks in my body. Sparkles of pleasure like tiny fireworks to enjoy.

He takes his pleasure the way he wants it. Slowly, and then faster. Slower again. I'm immersed in shimmering power and sweet, sunny pleasure. Basking in it.

Brae slams home, rhythm faltering when he's

close. Plunging deep, he holds himself there, cock jerking as he pours that heat inside me. His pleasure feels almost as good as my own. I savor it, rolling the flavor of it through my mind.

Lowering himself down to me, he kisses the under side of my jaw, drawing his lips up to my ear and then back to my mouth while he speaks. "The Goddess told you that you are where you are meant to be. And that means this too. No matter the scale."

"I don't want to believe it," I say, keeping my voice even. My emotions are close to the surface, and I'm afraid that they're going to come spilling over.

"Why not?"

"Because it doesn't make *sense*, Brae." I cover my face with my hands again, unable to look at him and see the compassion and understanding. "It doesn't. I can't say that I'm no one, or that I'm nothing. But choosing me—a human with no training and no real magical talent? It's hard to accept that that was a good idea."

Gently, Brae takes my wrists and pulls them away so that he can see my face. "How many decisions do you make in a day?"

"What?"

"How many? Even the little ones. Like what to wear or which way to sleep?"

I snort. "I probably can't count that high."

He smirks. "Neither can I. But imagine that, with every person, every fae. Every decision splitting the world into infinite facets. And the Goddess can see all of them. What makes you think that this wasn't planned a long time ago?"

"But—"

"She told you that she and Allwyn always make decisions that benefit us. That benefit the world. Even if you weren't a thought yet, she could have looked to the future and seen where you needed to be to stop this. There's a reason that you have magic.

"Wherever in your past that magic came from— even if it wasn't a plan—she saw that in you. We may not ever know why. And believe me I understand that it's frustrating as hell. But never assume that you're here by accident."

I latch on to the confidence pouring off him. He believes this with his entire being, and that's a little intoxicating. "What if I'm not good enough?"

"Did the Goddess ask you to be good enough?"

Pressing my lips together, I shake my head. He knows that she didn't. She didn't specifically ask me to do anything. But when I can feel her presence, I know that this is why I was gifted this magic. To save her. Or to try.

Brae kisses my forehead, and in that moment I'm

reminded of the fact that he used to be a priest. The kiss feels like a benediction and an absolution. A release from this fear and burden. "We will face this together," he says softly. "All of us. And we will do what we can, the best that we can. There are just as many possibilities in front of us as there were behind us."

Wrapping my arms around him, I pour my love into him through that shimmering thread between us. And my gratitude for the reassurance. "Should we tell the others?"

"It can wait till morning," he says, pulling the blanket up and over us and pulling me closer. "Rest. And hopefully no more dreams."

Closing my eyes, I sink into his magic. It feels like the sunset, lulling me into sleep and rest. I hope for no more dreams too.

CHAPTER TEN

KENT

I splash water over my face and scrub the sweat from my skin. I've been up for hours longer than everyone else in the house, because I haven't been able to sleep. This meeting has me nervous, and when I'm nervous I fall back into old habits. Push my body to the limit and gather as much information as I can.

Even though we've been on guard and looked everywhere, there's about a thousand ways that this meeting could go wrong. And I'm the most vulnerable—now the only one without magic. But like hell am I not going. I want this woman to know that I am not afraid, and I'm not going to stay behind a shield because of my humanity.

That doesn't stop the possibilities and hypothetical situations from spinning in my head. Too many years as a cop, constantly thinking of the way things can go wrong and assuming the worst. Too many cases—both professional and personal—tracking down fae that have done horrifying things. I know better than most that the fae aren't perfect, and even though not all the myths are true, enough of them are to make me cautious.

I put on the clothes that we've selected. This is the first time we're meeting Ariana on our terms, and our one chance to make an impression. The truth is that impressions matter, and a show of force and will is one of our best defenses. Along with one other thing.

Something I'm not going to show Kari.

I finish lacing up the corseted vest that many fae seem to prefer for formalwear. I imagine I'll have to get used to wearing this, even if I can't breathe. And then I grab the gun that I've had stashed here since we first arrived. I've never had reason to fire it and the ash bullets that it contains, which was specifically designed to harm the fae. Honestly, I hoped I would never have reason to touch it again.

I think that this is a pretty good fucking reason.

No one knows what makes ash painful to the fae, and until now I've never thought to ask. The only thing that ever mattered to me when I had the gun was that it gave me an advantage, and with the creatures I was hunting I needed every advantage that I could get.

Knocking on Aeric's door, I wait. If anyone agrees with me about this, it's going to be him. He's dressed too, clothes dark and emphasizing the green tones of his skin while showing his strength. It's a good image for the impression we're trying to send. "I need to talk to you for a moment."

I register his surprise before he steps aside and lets me in. We've become more friendly in these past weeks, but seeking him out isn't exactly a habit. "If things go south, do we have a plan?"

"Get Kari to safety at all costs."

I take a breath, to make sure that I say this in a way that's not going to make him punch me in the face. "You remember how we met?"

He rolls his eyes. "Kind of hard to forget that introduction, Kent."

Actions are better than words in this case. I pull the gun out of the back of my waistband and hold it out on my palm, making sure it doesn't look like I'm brandishing it.

Aeric stares at it for a moment, and shakes his head. "If anyone in Allwyn knew you had that, the absolute mountain of shit—"

"I know," I say. "There's a reason I haven't told anyone. Frankly I wish that it would have gathered dust for the rest of my existence."

"There aren't exactly a lot of laws here. But I think the ones against ash weapons are the only laws that are acknowledged in every Kingdom."

"Why ash?"

He shrugs. "Cerys. The Goddess. It could have been anything, but she didn't want to create a power imbalance the way there was before. So she gave us that weakness. Ash trees are not native to Allwyn. Just a way for humans to more effectively defend themselves, if it comes to that. So she made it poisonous to fae and the Gods alike." He's still staring at the weapon. "You said that you've killed fae before."

I keep my face even. "I have." It was not an easy nor a pleasant experience. "In the course of doing my job, sometimes I didn't have a choice."

"And that's the only time you've killed?"

He's not looking at the gun anymore. He's looking at me, and I meet his gaze. But I don't say anything. There's nothing to say, because it's none of his business. That's not a part of my life I'll share with the other fae in this house unless I have no other choice. "I came to ask if you think it's a good idea. To have it for this meeting."

Crossing to the chair in front of his tool bench, Aeric sits. "We've never talked about the possibility of harming fae offensively. That's a discussion we need to have. Particularly since Ariana is controlling fae."

I tuck the gun back into my pants. "It's not ideal."

"No fucking kidding," he says, pulling out one of

his knives and spinning it. It's an instinctual movement. "But you're right."

"I can't stop thinking about what we don't know."

He's silent for long minutes, absently throwing the knife. I lean against one of the bed posts and wait. I'm on unfamiliar territory here, and I trust his judgement.

Finally, Aeric sighs. "Take it. But only use it if absolutely necessary."

"That's the plan. If I have to," I say, "I know where I'm aiming."

His face is grim. "Me too."

"Even armed, I don't like this."

Standing, he leads me out of the door. He doesn't have to speak his agreement, I already know that he feels the same. I just want this to be over.

CHAPTER ELEVEN

KARI

My stomach is still bubbling with nerves and nausea as I dress. I'm clinging to Brae's confidence, and Aeric's steadiness. Thank the Goddess.

Brae volunteered to relay the information from last night, and the plan. Fine with me. I don't want to relive that. The primal power coming from beneath that stone, and the simple, callous nature of Ariana's mission. There's no way I'm going to be able to eat anything this morning, even though the house is filled with the smell of baking pancakes and sugar.

It's unfair that my mouth is watering and I know I'm not going to be able to eat. But in a way it's sweet, like the magic of the house is apologizing for what I'm feeling and trying to ply me with sugar. Which I appreciate, and will hopefully be stuffing my face with later.

Because I'm going to have to do all the talking. Otherwise the show of power and strength that we're projecting will mean nothing. Me and my five silent guards, willing to do anything in order to protect me.

Yeah, food is off the table.

The dress I'm wearing for this is one of the batch that Kaya sent. It's laced with wards and protection charms. I'm confident in my ability to shield myself, but when it comes to Ariana I'm not going to take any chances. It also helps that I really love this dress. Deep blue with a plunging neckline and a sharp enough cut that I feel badass. But also soft enough to make me feel pretty. Either way I'm standing tall in it, and I'll take what I can get right now.

I stand in front of the mirror, looking at myself, and I try to see what they see. The men in this house, and the Goddess that chose me. But I'm just…me. Who I've always been.

The idea that I was always chosen is both comforting and terrifying at once. On the one hand, I would know without a doubt that I'm on the right course. But on the other hand the idea of a fate this vast makes me wonder if I'll measure up to it.

For a moment I close my eyes, reaching deep and lifting magic into my fingertips. I make it visible. Combined gold and violet, shimmering and shifting in my hand like a little swirling cloud. I need to trust this, and trust my mates.

It's time.

Brae is on his way up the stairs when I step out of my room. The shock that rolls through him followed by his distinctly male appreciation and desire make me grin at him. I'm already used to the external sensing of their feelings, and it's not nearly as intrusive as I feared it might be. They seem to distance themselves when not needed, and intensify when I reach for them. I wonder if that's part of the magic?

"If you can sense my feelings, does it bother you if I tell you how beautiful you are?" he asks, stopping in front of me and bowing.

"You're not too bad yourself." The fitted clothes show off every inch of him, and the purple highlights his golden complexion. I find myself torn at moments like these. Wanting to drag one of them away to a quiet corner and barricade myself with them for nothing but hours of lazy and indulgent pleasure. But there are bigger things than sex, even if Brae's pants make it clear I'm not the only one with the thought.

The rest of them are gathered in the entryway, arrayed in powerful clothing. Similar enough that it almost looks like a uniform, with touches that reflect each of them. If they knew how they looked to me right now—practically lickable—maybe they'd wear this more often.

I suppress my smile when Brae and Aeric look at

me, both of them catching the thought. But I don't comment. The mood in the air is heavy, and we're all eager to get on with it.

"Kari does the talking," Brae says, looking at me. "Unless she tells us otherwise. Right?"

"Right."

Urien is the one to draw the portal in front of us, laced in azure light that shatters into facets in the air. Thankfully for my swimming stomach, we step directly through the portal where we need to go, and not through twenty. Ariana already knows that we're coming. Why bother to hide?

I was unconscious when I left this place, and it's the first time I've seen the true aftermath of the explosion. An entirely flat circle of ash and dust a hundred feet across. Jagged stones scattered beyond that, the equivalent of fallen trees here. Pure destruction.

Little curls of dust reach up from under our feet when we step onto the surface. Looking at this—if I didn't know what happened—I would be shocked that anyone survived.

Brae and Aeric place themselves close at my shoulders. In spite of the seriousness I fight a smile and Kent winks at me. Their protective mate instincts are in full force. It's sweet, and it might just keep me alive.

A flash of light blinds me for a moment, and Ariana is there, along with Kiaran. Four other fae as well, though the dead looks on their faces tell me they're under her control. They are here to mirror my entourage.

I try not to look at Kiaran. As far as I know, Ariana does not know who he is to me—every one of our encounters is so brief that I haven't asked. But I see enough. He's taken, eyes shining with malevolent light stronger than I've ever seen it. A tinge of orangey red glows there. She's taking no chances with him.

I don't see the rush of illness coming. This isn't a curse or an attack, it's me. Ariana is wearing that same black dress that I can't shake from my memory. That same red lipstick and smile. She's a ghost that stepped straight out of my worst nightmare, and she knows it. She did it on purpose. It takes everything in me not to double over.

A tiny trace of power caresses down my spine. Urien's power, cool and refreshing like the night. They're standing with me. I am not alone. The coolness of that touch snaps my mind back to the present, and I'm able to look at her. She smiles slowly, like a predator cornering prey that has nowhere to go.

"You look better than the last time I saw you,

Kari."

Breathe in. Out. Don't let her see the fear. The power inside me pulses in response, a subtle reminder of why she wants me in the first place. "No thanks to you."

She laughs, bright and fake and easy. "Still angry about that? You survived. And it seems did very well for yourself." Her eyes flit between the men arrayed around me. "Though I wonder why you needed to bring them all with you? You're the only one with an invitation."

Beside me, I can sense everyone go on high alert. They may have agreed to stay silent, but they'll act the second anything goes wrong.

"I know what you're planning to do," I say. "And I can't let you do it."

Ariana tilts her head. She's studying me, smile gone. "Oh? How are you going to stop me?"

"Did you think it would be that simple? I'd just show up and volunteer to let you take me? Kill me or worse?"

She looks at our surroundings and shrugs. "After what happened here, I thought you might see that it's the easier option."

I stay silent, fighting the urge to move. Instead I let myself become stone. Impervious to her and her manipulation.

She's the one who moves, slowly walking through the fine debris leaving a trail of footsteps behind her. "No matter what you think of me, this must be done. Even after all the trouble you've caused, I'm willing to look the other way. If you surrender your power, that is."

I don't rise to the bait. Don't show hope. We both know that there's not a chance that she'll let me get out of this alive if she has any say in the matter. Ariana is not one to leave witnesses. The trail of human women she left behind before me is proof enough of that.

When she finally focuses on me, the blow she aims makes me gasp. It bounces harmlessly off my barrier woven of gold, but the amount of power she already has is staggering. Far more than I remember feeling from her. Not even Kiaran has that kind of power, and she was only testing me. No matter if the magic is stolen or not, if she gathered everything she had and pointed it straight at me, I'm no longer sure that I would walk away.

A ghost of a smile crosses her lips. "You are fascinating."

"Given what you do to things that fascinate you, that's not a compliment."

Her smile now is the most genuine one I've ever seen, and it's terrifying. Ariana is stunningly beautiful, and in another life I could see her in the Carnal Court, finding love and happiness. How did she end up here? Was that fate too?

In spite of myself, I glance at Kiaran. How much of this is he aware of through her control?

"We can stand here forever and banter," she says, stopping directly across from me in her wandering. "Or we can get to the point. Do you accept my invitation to surrender?"

"No."

Ariana faces me square on, hands folded delicately behind her back. Her face is peaceful. "I expected as much. And I came prepared with a counter-offer."

All it takes is a flick of her wrist to make my world fall apart. A portal swirls open beside her, the brutal lines of magic cutting through the air like wounds. Bright red light pulling back to reveal Emma.

She's unconscious, suspended in the air. Spirals of ruby energy coil around her like a snake. It roams over her skin, possessive and poisonous. The sight is eerily familiar.

I'm nothing but deja vu and rage. I know what happens when you're like that. When she has you. I lunge for the portal without thinking, and Aeric is the one that holds me back from diving through.

Everything looks red to me—the same color as that portal and the magic touching my friend and Ariana's blood that I'm going to scatter on this pile of ash we're standing on. "Let her go." I don't recognize the feral sound that is my own voice.

All pretense and friendliness is gone from Ariana's manner. "See, Kari? You could have made this simple. It could have just been you. No one else had to get hurt. But you're predictable. All you humans. So loyal."

I fight against Aeric's hold. I'm going to kill her now. I can. Magic boils under my skin, burning with the need to hunt and harm and kill. Let this be over. "It's me you want."

"It is," Ariana admits, calmly snapping her fingers. The portal to Emma collapses into thin air. Terror wraps my heart in a fist, squeezing until I can barely breathe. *No*.

She opens her hands in an apologetic gesture. "But you said no. I guess we'll see what matters the most to you."

"Kari," the voice is Brae's, soft enough that only I can hear. I brush it aside. I don't want to be in check right now, I want to burn, and I know that I can. Maybe it would be worth it to take her with me.

"You have three days," Ariana says. "Before she dies."

"If you kill her—"

"I'm not going to kill her," she says, cutting me off. "You are. If you refuse me again." A tiny smile. "I never took you for a murderer, Kari."

I am a creature born of fury and pain. Nothing more. Power spirals from my fingertips almost before the thought enters my head. A burst meant to incinerate and end.

The sound of it is sharp, echoing in my ears, and then the power bounces into nothing off a wall of blue flame. Kiaran stumbles backwards, shoulder bloody. It's only a second later that I see the gun in Kent's hand. An ash gun. The weapon he used to carry as a police officer. Deadly to fae.

And Kent is a perfect shot.

Horror and dread crack through me like a bomb. That bullet would have gone straight into her heart if Kiaran hadn't jumped in front of her, completely willing to sacrifice himself for her. And we would have lost Emma completely.

Blood pours from Kiaran's wound, soaking through the clothes, but he looks unfazed. Like he didn't even feel it. The other fae with them haven't even moved. *Please, Goddess, let him be all right.*

For the first time, I see Ariana look shaken.

Her portal whips open behind her, a gaping hole into darkness. Her dark eyes seek out mine. There is death in that gaze, and absolutely no mercy. "Now you have two days."

She disappears into mist, Kiaran and the rest of the fae filing behind her. They're gone in seconds, leaving behind nothing but echoes and my own madness.

"No." The word falls from me like a stone. No no no. All I can hear are those echoes of that. Aeric releases me, and my legs don't hold my weight. I sink into the silt, the feeling of it between my fingers keeping me grounded.

Brae is at their portal within seconds, fingertips tracing the air and searching for the remnants of the path.

Fingers brush my back and I recoil. "Don't touch me," I breathe into the dirt. "Don't touch me."

"Kari." Feet appear directly in front of my eyes. It's Verys crouching down. "We'll find her."

"I could have found her now. I could have made it through." I glare at Aeric. "Why did you stop me?"

"We don't know that she has Emma. It could be a trap or an illusion. The instant you went through that portal, there was no guarantee that you were coming back."

I turn to Kent, still seething and too angry to listen to reason. "You could have killed him. And if you had killed her Emma would be gone forever."

"I won't apologize for trying to protect you and end this fast."

Brae steps away from the place they disappeared with a hiss. "She was careful. We can't follow them from here."

"We need to find her. *Now*." Panic bordering on hysteria sticks to my insides like glue. I can't take a full breath. All I can see is Emma bent and suspended in the air, dying. That magic is slowly draining the life from her, and I know exactly how that feels.

The portal that Urien slices through the air is more sharp than the others I've seen. "Quickly," he says. "We need to move quickly and carefully. First make sure she's really gone."

Please. I release the word like a prayer into the sky. I want nothing more than to appear at Emma's apartment and find her on the couch watching a movie with ice cream.

But if she's not there, I did this. Emma never asked for this—doesn't deserve that kind of hell—being trapped in her own mind. I allow Aeric to help me to my feet and follow Urien through the portal, grasping onto that thread of hope that she's still safe. That Ariana is bluffing, and a liar.

If she's not, I'm not sure what I'll do.

CHAPTER TWELVE

———

KARI

Everything looks perfectly fine outside Emma's apartment, but it's not. Even I can feel that. There's an almost supernatural stillness in this hallway. Almost like everything is trying just a little too hard to be normal. The magic coming off her door is just like what I felt when Ariana set my shop on fire: magic that feels like someone digging their fingers into a painful bruise without mercy.

I don't need to see inside to know that she's gone. There's no way that kind of magic is coming off her door and she's still in there and alive. Beside me, Brae is rigid with tension, and what little strength and calm I've managed to hold on to is almost gone.

Brae waves a hand, and the glamour that's been sewn over her door disappears. It is pure destruction. The door is shattered into pieces, wood blown everywhere. That's all I see before I turn to the wall, hiding my face, using it for support. This can't be happening. It can't.

Pain cracks through my chest, breaking me, unmaking everything I thought I was. "No," I whisper. The first tear falls, and I can't stop the rest of them. Hands made of dread and devastation are crushing me. "It's not real," I manage to say. "It's not. Tell me it's not real."

"We're going to find her," someone says softly, and that only makes the tears come harder.

It's my fault that she's gone. All because of me. If I wasn't here, if I wasn't *fated*, if I hadn't loved and chosen these men. Emma would be safe and nothing would be wrong. She would be on a date with a man that makes her smile and not broken and bleeding, serving as nothing more than a battery and a pawn in Ariana's sick need for magic and control.

She was taunting me. Teasing me with reminders of my own pain and forcing it onto someone else. Because she could. Because she knows that I still flash back to those powerless moments in fear and taste her poison on my tongue. Still see the terror in my mates' eyes when they acknowledge that I was close to death. Because she somehow knew exactly how to strike me in my heart and make me bleed.

Hands cover mine on the wall, body pressing against my back. Aeric. I fight against his grip, but he holds on. "Let go," he whispers in my ear. "Let it go."

The sound that comes out of me is ugly and desperate. Everything comes out of me at once. Pain and anger, grief and fear. A torrent of emotion spilling outward that I'm powerless to stop or control. Air is jagged in my chest, every breath like a knife to the heart. But Aeric is holding me upright. Safe. And so I am able to release it.

I press my forehead against the wall, fingers clawing at the plaster. Aeric weaves our fingers together and wraps his arms around me. Pinning my hands safely against my body and holding me at once. A soft kiss brushes the back of my neck, tasting of safety and acceptance and sorrow. That's what I feel through the bond from him. Sorrow. A wish that he could take the pain away, and a deeper, driving anger towards Ariana and everything she's done.

There's no way for me to tell how long I stand there, bound and held by him. Everything passes up and through, and every last bit of feeling that I've kept buried for weeks is exorcised. When it finally stops, I'm empty. My heart feels like that blasted patch of ash that we just came from.

This is what it will be like if I ever lose one of them. Worse than this. A pain that changes who you are. My breath hitches, and Aeric pulls me harder against his body. "Breathe for me," he says so quietly that it's only a ghost of a whisper. I try, and my whole body shudders in response. "I'm going to turn you around," he says, voice still quiet.

"But you will move no more than that. Do you understand?"

Slowly, I bow my head in agreement. In this moment, that control feels like a blessing. Even moving feels like too much. His hands shift on my waist, releasing my hands and turning me to face him. I close my eyes, not wanting to see any other faces. His body is still crowding mine, securing me to the wall and keeping me standing. "Look at me."

I press my eyes shut harder, a few stray tears leaking. A thumb brushes away the wetness, and the tenderness in the touch nearly wrecks me all over again. "Kari." Gentle command is in the tone. I open my eyes, and we're alone. A barrier of swirling jade smoke surrounds us, shielding us from view.

There's no judgement or fear in Aeric's gaze. Just love and understanding. "This is not your fault."

"Yes it is," I say, voice breaking. "Emma would be safe if it weren't for me."

"Is it your fault that Ariana attacked you? Your fault that you were given and inherited magic?"

I shake my head. I couldn't have stopped those things.

"Then how is this your fault?"

The point he's trying to make is clear, but that doesn't change the guilt that's weighing on my heart like a boulder is chained there. "We are going to find Emma," he says. "Nothing is going to happen to her."

"You can't know that."

"No," he says. "But I believe it."

Moving with that same careful slowness, Aeric slides his hand up my spine to that familiar position where his hand is in my hair. Barely tugging, but enough for my stomach to sink and my mind to relax into familiar territory. Yielding to my mate. "I am going to kiss you," he says. "And then I'm going to drop the barrier. There is no shame in this. No apology. We've all lost things—more than you know. And after that, we're going to find her. If you think you're going to fall apart again, tell me. You know I'll feel it. You will not be alone."

"I don't want to do that again," I say, aware that my throat is raw with emotion and still unshed tears.

He pulls my head back just enough to brush his mouth with mine. This kiss is not about arousal. It's comfort and refuge and the promise that he will hold me, no matter what happens. "We both know that want and need are not the same, Kari. And there is no shame in needing to break sometimes."

The smoke around us disappears, and despite him telling me it's fine, I fight the wave of embarrassment. The only thing I'm greeted with is touch, drawn into a circle of arms and reassurance. Silent in solidarity.

I feel when I'm ready, the subtle shift in the air settling. The tiny thread of determination I feel is the thing I hold on to when I open my eyes. Every one of them is touching me, their warmth seeping into my skin and keeping me sane. I don't deserve these men.

Brae is the first one to speak. "I need something to track Emma," he says. "Something personal. There are signs of a struggle, but nothing more than that. No blood. Just some broken glass, and the door."

"I'll repair the door," Urien says. "If you don't need the traces."

"Go ahead."

They let me go when I step away and into the apartment. It's just like I remember it, barring the debris of the entryway, and the shattered dishes in the kitchen. That must have been where she was when they took her. I steer myself away from the thought, and take some tissues from a nearby box to wipe my face.

Something personal. I can do that. "How deep do you need it to be?" I ask Brae, my voice still weak.

"The stronger it is, the easier it will be to track," he says. "If she had magical abilities, it would be different. But for humans without them—" he cuts himself off. "Deep."

I know what I need.

In Emma's bedroom, I go to the closet. I'm crossing my fingers that she still keeps it where I remember it to be. On the top shelf, a small box that I'll never forget. We lived together for a while, Emma, Odette and I, when we were newer to the city. That box never left her bedside table.

It's an unassuming thing, just a round hatbox, designed with some abstract flowers. But to Emma, it's everything. These are the mementos she's kept over the years—only things that mean something to her. She hasn't had the easiest life, and the tokens she chose to keep reminded her of the best parts of it.

Quickly, I set it on the bed, and open it. The toe shoes I'm looking for are sitting right on top. Mangled nearly to death with use and faded with age. They're the first pair of toe shoes that she ever owned, and she always said putting them on was the first time in her life that she had felt true freedom. I take them, and put the rest of the box back where I found it.

As I'm going back to the living room something snags my eye. A picture of the three of us. One of those silly mall photo booth pictures. We're all scrunched up together and nearly crying from laughter. The picture is tucked into the side of her vanity mirror, and it hits me all at once. Shit.

"Will these work?" I ask, holding the shoes out to Brae when I enter the room.

He holds them gently. "Perfectly. The connection here is nearly permanent."

"They're really important to her."

"No harm will come to them. I swear it," he says with a hint of a smile.

Across the room I lock eyes with Kent. "We need to go."

Eyebrows rise into his hairline. "Where?"

"Odette."

Darkness crashes across his features. "Fuck."

"Yeah."

Emma is not the only bargaining chip that Ariana has access to. Odette was just as exposed the day of the fire, and it would be just like Ariana to hold back a second hostage. The rest of the guys immediately pick up on the urgency. Urien takes my hand. "Show me where."

I picture the street outside Odette's apartment, and I'm hoping that she's home. If not, I'll break down the door at the rehearsal space. She needs to know, and I need to be sure that she's safe. We step out onto the sidewalk, and I don't give a flying fuck that people are staring at us as we pass through a gash in time and space. And they are staring at us.

The code to Odette's building is something I've had memorized for years, and we quickly escape inside. Writhing impatience makes me fidget in the elevator all the way up to the seventh floor, and when the doors open I can take my first inhale of relief. I don't sense any dark magic here. I ring the doorbell, and nearly sink to my knees when I hear footsteps on the other side.

Odette opens the door, eyes going wide in shock when she sees the six of us standing on the other side. And then she pulls me into a hug without a second thought. "Hey! I'm so sorry I couldn't come visit the other day, but I wanted to. I'm glad you're here though, I could use some of your sage dancer advice."

That's how long it takes her to realize that I'm not hugging her back with the same exuberance. She pulls back and looks at me, sudden wariness in her eyes. "Kari, what's wrong."

I swallow, trying to get the words past the lump in my throat. "Emma is gone."

CHAPTER THIRTEEN

AERIC

I step out onto the New York sidewalk, the air slipping into coolness as the sun starts to fade. Kent and Brae are right behind me, and Kari is still upstairs, consoling her friend and explaining what the hell happened. I needed a fucking second to breathe.

The pain coming off Kari back there was almost more than I was able to take. If I could rip that pain out of her soul and carry it in mine I would do it in a heartbeat. There are some things that I'll never be able to forget, even in my long life. Parts of the war. The moment that my magic changed its allegiance. A handful of happy moments, and sad ones too. The moment that we met Kari and the moment that I thought she was gone.

Never in my life will I forget the sound of my mate weeping and crying for her friend, afraid that she might have cost Emma her life. We've been so wrapped up in each other, and in her getting to know the five of us, that we haven't talked much about Kari's relationships with her friends and family. Basic stories. But that kind of grief speaks to a deeper friendship than I imagined.

Kari, Odette, and Emma danced together for years, and for the first time I'm understanding exactly what that means. She thinks of them as sisters in the way I think of Brae and Verys as my brothers. We fought together, and that bonded us in a way that no one else will understand. It's the same for Kari.

Regardless, I feel sick. Even now, through that glimmering, tenuous connection, she's hurting. I haul in a breath, trying to cleanse the horror from my chest and stomach. I lean over, leaning on my legs. This is not something I have experience with—taking control in the midst of pain. I love commanding Kari's pleasure. This—

I'm so fucking grateful the Goddess allowed us this. We've already practiced this dynamic, and I know deep in my gut that it's one of the only things that helped her. The fact that she *knew* I could and would lead her. Hold her. Make sure she was safe enough to breathe and feel. And I will do it again if she needs me to. Anytime. Every time.

But my heart still hurts for her, wishing she didn't need me to do that.

"Are you all right?" Kent asks.

All I have is honesty. "I don't know."

Brae's gaze is on the street around us, ever on guard. "That was brutal."

I take one more deep breath in before straightening. "It's going to be brutal. As long as Ariana is in the picture."

"My shot was clean," Kent says, pissed as hell. "This could have been over."

Brae sighs. "He's enchanted. I could feel it coming off of all of them. He probably doesn't even remember that he saved her life, or if he's conscious in there he has no options."

"Will he live?" Being so close to Kari's most recent dose of pain, I don't want to see what happens if one of her mates is gone too.

Kent gives a curt nod. "From where I was standing, yes. He got lucky, but where I saw the bullet land should be simple enough to remove and heal."

"It's ash," I say. "So it won't be simple. But even if Kari is angry about it now, she'll be grateful that he's alive."

I can see the tension rolling off Kent. His arms are crossed, shoulders are high, and he's examining every person passing on the street like they're an immediate threat. "How did they get through? I was with Verys when he warded that apartment. I saw him do it, and he didn't skimp on the good stuff."

Brae leans against the front of the building. "I'm not shocked. Could you feel the magic back there?"

Kent shrugs. "A little, but not any more than I sense when we're at home."

"Ariana tested her shield with a strike that could have *leveled* all of us. That kind of power is rare, and I've only seen it a couple times. Once yesterday with Kari. But the magic isn't hers. She's stolen it. But if she brought that much magic and brute-forced the wards, they would have snapped."

Kent looks pale. "So she could have come in at any time?"

"One more way she was toying with us," I say.

Reaching out through the bond, I send soothing feelings to Kari. Comfort and support. For a moment, that hurt I can feel lessens. Looking over at Brae, I wonder if he's experiencing it the same way? My initial reaction of jealousy passed faster than I thought it would. Last night I felt pleasure pouring off Kari in waves, and even knowing that Brae was the one fucking her didn't bother me. Because she was happy. Cared for. Safe. And the sudden, blinding realization that her mating with Brae does not invalidate our bond. It only adds to it.

Already, I can feel that things are different than they were in my family. We...work. It won't always be simple or easy, but I have faith that we'll be able to work through whatever comes our way. If we can survive it.

"What do we do now?" I ask.

Kent blows out a breath. "Odette needs protection. I could make a case for the police here, but if Ariana comes for her, they won't be able to do anything."

"Urien should be able to dispatch some guards from the Court, at least temporarily. Other than setting up wards on her apartment, I'm not sure there's much else we can do for her. She can't come with us, that would be too dangerous for her. And she's in the middle of the biggest show of her life."

"We'll get those guards here as soon as possible, then."

Brae holds Emma's toe shoes in his hand. "Other than that, we just need to find her."

"You have a direction?" Kent asks.

"I can get us close."

None of us say anything about what we're really thinking: what happens when we find her?

CHAPTER FOURTEEN

KARI

Odette is pale while I tell her what happened. It takes a while to fill her in on the whole story, and she's quiet for most of it. Staring down at her hands and anywhere but at me. "I'm going to do everything I can to get her back. I swear it."

"I know," she says quietly before she reaches for my hand. "I'm glad that she doesn't have you too."

"I'm so sorry. I never should have let her come to visit. It's my fault. They'll tell you it's not, but it is."

Odette shakes her head, blonde curls falling around her shoulders. "You're not responsible for the actions of the bitch trying to torture you. I feel terrible that I didn't know! I just assumed that she was tired from rehearsal or missed my texts. After what happened to you I should have checked on her."

I wrap my arms around her and pull her into a hug. We rest in each other for a moment. "What can I do?" she asks.

"Be the best Odette you can possibly be."

She rolls her eyes. "I'm serious, Kari."

"So am I. You don't know how much I wish I could bring you with me, but that just plays right into her hands. And as much fun as we'd have with the magical sleepover, I can't just lock you up inside our house in the middle of your tech week."

She stands up from the couch and starts to pace. "There are understudies for a reason."

"Odette, no."

The door to the apartment opens and quiet footsteps enter. The guys are back from outside. And I feel a tug in my chest—Aeric questioning if he can interject. I send back a confirmation. "Odette," he says, stepping closer. "We're going to set up protection around your apartment, and if you can, Urien, we would like you to dispatch guards. At least temporarily."

She goes pale again. "You think that's necessary?"

"We do," Brae says. "They will remain invisible. No one will know."

Odette hesitates for a minute, staring at the ground and tapping her foot. "Okay, yeah. It would make me feel better if they don't mind babysitting a human."

Urien just nods. "They will do as they're asked, and Verys and I just completed wards around your apartment. If anything happens, we'll know about it."

"But nothing will," I say firmly, glaring at the guys. "We're going to take care of it."

"We should go," Kent says quietly.

I look at Odette, fighting back the tears I thought were gone. "I'm so sorry. I'm so sorry. I don't want to risk being here longer than we need to be."

I hug her again, and this time she returns it fiercely. "If anything happens to you I'm going to fucking lose it," she whispers in my ear. Then she pulls back and looks at my men. "I know you all heard that. If you let anything happen to her I am coming to Allwyn and kicking *all* of your asses."

"That's the plan," Verys says.

I don't want to leave, and I find myself hesitating. "I'm going to get her back. I promise."

"Go, Kari," she says.

I only hesitate for another second before turning and walking through the door. Another hug would have broken me again. "Brae," I say when we step into the evening light. "Where are we going?"

"Back to the mansion. I'll track Emma as far as I can and—"

"Like hell," I say. "No."

"What?" he seems genuinely shocked.

I cross my arms and stare him down. "I'm going with you. I don't want us separated right now. Not when Ariana has every reason to pick us off one at a time. Let's go. Now. She thinks we're regrouping, let's go."

He matches my stare without flinching, and through our connection I don't feel anger, just consideration. Urien speaks. "She has a point."

"All right," he says. "Let's go."

Cold relief pours down my back like ice water. I'm not going to just sit and let them do this without me. If we're doing it, we're doing it together.

Emma's shoes are in one hand, and he draws a portal with the other. The light tracing the portal is white shot through with purple, and it opens onto a landscape that I've never seen before. It almost seems nonsensical.

Brae steps through first and I follow. The sky here is a pale grey, but I could swear I see it morphing into green as I watch. The rolling little hill of dirt we're standing on ends in a cliff of rock piercing the sky. But that cliff only seems to be ten feet wide, like a spire, with nothing similar within my view.

The portal collapses behind Kent, revealing an entire grove of trees that are burnt to a crisp. "Where are we?"

"The Wild Kingdom," Brae says with obvious distaste.

"What's here?"

"Anything," Urien says. "Everything. Things that don't fit into the other Kingdoms."

Brae starts walking to the left and I follow him. "There also happen to be very few laws here. I'm not surprised this is where she's hiding."

"And not a place we should draw undue attention," Verys says. But he draws the sword that's strapped across his back. I forgot that they were armed. They mask the weapons in the human realm so they don't get stopped by the police.

The ring of metal sounds again as the rest of them draw their swords. "I need a weapon," I say.

"You have one," Brae says. "Your magic is all you need. A weapon you're not familiar with is just as deadly as being unarmed."

Fair point. I draw power into my palms so I have it ready if I need it.

The things we pass don't make any sense. At least not next to each other. There's a patch of small red flowers that I swear smell like pizza. Trees that radiate stingy energy. A waterfall that runs backwards into nothing and fires that seem to pop into existence as they please.

It is beautiful, in its own way.

While we're walking, I double check my shield. It's become second nature now for me to hold it, and it's there without any holes. But I carefully expand it so that we're all contained within its bubble.

"We're close," Brae says.

But I can't see anything close to here that would count as a place to hide. "Where?"

Our immediate surroundings look like ice. There are a few hills obscuring the horizon with pools in random places, but no structures. When I reach out with magic I don't feel anything that's hidden either. "Brae?"

He closes his eyes, and it looks like he's listening hard. In my chest I feel his concentration and connection. "Below us," he finally says.

"There," Verys points. There's a depression in the ground near one of the hills, and it does look like it sinks further. Against this background of white ice and gray sky, Verys looks entirely in his element. I want to take pictures of him in monochrome, because they would be so beautiful.

There are so many things I want to do with them.

The men array themselves in front of me as we approach, and I let them. This isn't worth arguing about. The hole in the ground opens into a low cave, and I can just barely see it continue downwards under the earth. It's subtle, and I don't think I would have seen it at all without fae eyes. "She's down here?"

"Likely," Brae says. "I can't pinpoint her at this moment, but she's below the surface."

"What are we waiting for?" I step down into the cave. It's darker, but the light from the surface penetrates enough. The temperature has dropped—confirming the ice. This must be a glacier of some kind. A broken one if it ended up in the Wild Kingdom.

The tunnel curves down into darkness, and I push my magic out, trying to do what they do. Sense anything and everything that could be harmful. There's nothing. Just an empty tunnel of ice.

There's no way that Ariana has left herself unprotected. She's too careful. "I'm not getting anything."

The fae shake their heads. They aren't either. But that doesn't make any of them look calmer. Kent especially is looking around like he expects Ariana's fae to jump out from anywhere. "I don't like this."

"Something isn't right," Aeric agrees with him. "She would have defenses."

Pulling the magic from my fingers, I create a ball of light and toss it down the corridor, making the ice shimmer and shine. In places the surface is smooth and glassy and others it's jagged and cubic like stone.

Nothing at all seems out of place or strange, and it almost reminds me of Emma's hallway. Too perfect and too innocent. But there's no magic. An absence of it almost. There's *nothing*.

"It doesn't make sense," I say. "But maybe that's part of being in the Wild Kingdom?"

The tunnel curves to the right, and I take a step forward see around the corner, and I feel it before I see it.

A body slams into mine, crushing me to the ground as molten heat pours from the walls. My vision is nothing but brightness, and melting flame. Shouts and noise, the roaring of the explosion and fire suddenly filling the vacuum that was empty.

The flames extinguish as quickly as they appeared, and suddenly I can feel *everything*. Like I flipped a switch and suddenly there's light in a room that was dark.

Traps line the walls, and it's not just a tunnel, it's a maze. Beneath the surface is a tangled mess of these same paths. They merge and turn back on each other, and there are other entrances too. Holy shit.

Verys rolls off me. "Are you all right?"

"Fine," I say, a little winded from hitting the ground. "Are you?"

He nods, but I still see smoke coming from the back of his clothes. Singed, at the very least. I turn him around to inspect his back, and am relieved to find only surface damage to his clothes. I was so shocked, that my shield dropped when he pushed me down.

Brae is crouched near the partially melted wall, touching a glyph carved into the ice. It was not visible before. "Vanishing ward. Haven't seen one of these in a long time."

My limbs are buzzing with adrenaline. "At least we can sense everything now. That should make it easier."

"Kari," Verys says, "we can't do this."

I look at him. "Of course we can. We're here. We're ready. We can do this. They won't see us coming."

The look on Verys's face borders on angry, and that's not an expression he makes often. "We just broke the ward that hides everything. They very much will know we're coming."

"It's fine," I insist. "Right now they're surprised. We can do this. She's here, right?" I glance at Brae.

His eyes are troubled when he looks at me, but he nods. "See?"

"Kari—"

"Why did we come all the way here just to do nothing?" I let my power build in my body. "You're already armed. I will shield all of us if I need to. Let's go."

Verys grabs my arm before I can fully turn away

from him. "You need to stop. You're not thinking clearly and it's going to get you *and* Emma killed."

"I'm not—"

"*No.*" His voice rings through the tunnel, clear as a bell and scattering echoes off the melted walls. "We need a plan. And one that's better than just walking in some place we haven't seen because you're confident it will work. We need more weapons. We need *power*. Everything here was hidden with magic none of us can sense, and you have no idea if there's anything more hidden."

Not once in the time I've known him have I ever heard Verys yell. My heart stutters in my chest. We're so close. I can't just walk away.

"You're not walking away," he says, answering the question I hadn't realized that I'd spoken out loud. "Emma is safe until the deadline that Ariana set. And we need to prepare. We won't be successful if we do this now." He lowers his voice again. "You know that if you walk in there that I'm going to walk after you, but you need to understand that doing this is far more likely to end badly."

"What if she kills her anyway? Because we came early?" I say, holding back the panic that's threatening to drown me. If I made this mistake...

"She won't." It's Kent's voice from my left. "As

callous as it sounds, Ariana needs her as the bargaining chip."

I meet Verys's eyes, and in them I find compassion. "I'm sorry."

Lifting my chin with his finger, he kisses me lightly, and I do feel myself threatening to fall apart again. "You never have to apologize to me for loyalty."

Brae cuts a portal open to the front of the mansion, and I don't fight when Verys guides me through it. I feel ill walking away from Emma like that, but he's right. If it's more dangerous, I can't risk her life. Even if that means leaving her in torment longer.

I send up a prayer to the Goddess that she can hang on.

CHAPTER FIFTEEN

KARI

Urien disappears as soon as we get back to arrange for Odette's protection, and I retreat to my bedroom and lock the door. It's the first time that I've used the lock since I started living here, but I need to take a moment for myself.

I'm restless. Manic energy slithers under my skin. Now that I've tasted action, it feels wrong for me to stay still. When I danced full time I felt the same. Never staying in the same space. Always practicing. Always improving.

Even after I fell I pushed myself too hard. I was so desperate to get back to where I'd been before that I damaged myself. That's an uncomfortable pattern to recognize in your own behavior.

Brae, Aeric, and Verys don't talk about their time in the fae war. I can see that it hurts when they do, and I don't have the heart to push them when I see it. But I would be foolish to think that they don't know what they're doing, and tactical retreat can be a good strategy.

I force myself to lie down, and not move. Perfectly still, until the writhing energy subsides. It's painful when it goes, leaving me empty with nothing to mask the sadness and the terror. But I still don't move. I let everything pass through me, until I feel clear and calm. As much as I can be.

Tentatively, I reach for that bright core of magic inside me. I don't pull it out to use it. I just touch it.

"Hi," I say. It feels more real if I say the words out loud. "If you can hear me, please keep Emma safe until I can get there. Please."

I could keep on talking and asking the Goddess for help, but right now that's the only prayer that matters to me. For a long while I stay there, making sure I don't move. Resting. I can hear voices downstairs in the living room. The guys talking, and hopefully coming up with the plan I didn't.

From Aeric and Brae I'm feeling two different things. Aeric is radiating cool determination. For a moment I seem to pull his connection to the forefront, and I wonder if there's any way that he feels I'm focusing on him. It's almost like being touched by his magic, but not quite.

Brae is equally determined, but he's got a fair bit of worry there too. Without him in front of me I'm unable to know if the worry is for me, Emma, or all of us combined. There's every chance that one of us won't make it out alive out of this, and that has me worried too.

What is it like to actually want someone dead?

I've never really to stopped to think about the strong possibility that that is what this magic is for. But taking a life—my stomach rolls at the thought. The same way that new, fresh, panic grips me whenever I imagine one of us dying. There are too many things that we haven't experienced together.

Including not being mated to everyone.

Rolling off the bed, I shake the stiffness from my limbs and go downstairs. Everyone is there, and they quiet when I enter the room. Urien is first to speak. "There are two fae watching Odette until further notice."

One of the weights lifts of my chest. "Thank you." Sitting down across from them, I look around at each of them before speaking. "There are things we need to talk about."

Aeric speaks like he's been reading my mind. I guess in a way he has. "About killing?"

"Yeah."

"With the exception of Ariana, we can try to avoid it. I don't think there's a way to promise, but those fae we saw with her were not conscious. We'll do our best."

"Good."

I clear my throat and look at Verys. In spite of everything, the words bring a smile to my face. "You mentioned power. I'm assuming you mean powering up through sex?"

"I did. But you know we'd never force you to do that."

Aeric chuckles. "We've raised magic by ourselves plenty of times in our lives."

"Verys, Urien, I want to seal my bond with you tonight."

If a speck of dust fell onto the floor in this moment you would be able to hear it. "Is it the right time?" Urien asks.

"The right time is when we choose, and that's now. We're walking in there, and she's going to try to kill us. You. She won't hesitate. And I don't want to go in there without being bonded to all of you."

It feels strange, to talk about something so intimate so clinically. "I'll meet you upstairs."

I cross to Aeric, who's staring hard at the floor in front of him. The stab of jealousy from him was fierce and strong, but already it's smoothing out. Leveling. Easing. "Are you all right?"

He smiles at me, and despite the fact that I still find tightness and wariness in our connection his expression is open. He takes my hand and holds it. "I'll be fine."

"Okay."

I'm standing there in front of them, and it's been a while since I've felt this kind of tension with them. An awkwardness that I can't seem to shake. Maybe that's what battle-planning does. You're all dealing with it in your own way and you can't give more than you're able. By the end of the night, I plan on that tension being entirely erased.

Verys and Urien are standing together in my bedroom, waiting, and that awkwardness rolls its shoulders again. I clear my throat, unsure about how to start something like this. The other two times have felt like a natural extension of things. "You want to do this together? You could…take turns."

Reaching out, Verys catches me by the wrist. "Breathe, Kari. I don't need to feel the bond to see that you're freaking out."

He kisses me hard. Familiar. Safe. Something that we've absolutely done before, and I love it. My body responds before I can, and I wrap my arms around him. I've missed Verys's body more than I realized. Part of balancing between so many partners. Urien is behind me now, and I'm reminded of that morning that Kiaran appeared. When I woke up between the two of them. It didn't feel unnatural then, and there's no reason for it to feel that way now.

I lean into their combined embrace and breathe. "Together?" I ask.

Urien kisses my neck at the same time that Verys steals another from my lips. "That's fine with me."

CHAPTER SIXTEEN

AERIC

I stride into Kent's room and toss the sword at him before he's even fully paying attention, but he catches out of the air, looking slightly alarmed. "Is this the new way that you say hello?"

"Sparring," I say. "Now."

He looks at me for a second. "All right."

Usually we spar in the courtyard, but that's too close. Instead I walk outside into the darkening trees, and I don't wait for us to be fully ready before I attack, launching at him as soon as he steps outside. Kent manages to parry my blows, but barely. It feels good to move like this, falling back into old patterns and things that I can rely on completely.

Kari's violet light is a flame in my chest. Growing brighter as she starts to receive pleasure. And I don't hate the feeling. I really don't. I love that she's enjoying herself. But I can't shake that gnawing feeling in my gut that this is where it falls apart. Where everyone suddenly is fighting for her and everyone is unhappy.

She doesn't deserve to feel that from me right now, so I need to beat the living hell out of something. Kent will do just fine.

He grunts as he blocks a blow to his side, backing up so my next strike falls wide. "Okay," he says. "Time to talk."

"I didn't start sparring with you to talk."

"And I didn't sign up to be the practice dummy for whatever you're taking out on me. So tell me what the hell's going on."

I pull back, spinning the sword in my palm. "I have trouble with this."

Kent goes on the offensive, a fast attack from above and then my left as he spins. He's really getting better at this. "Define 'this.'"

I sidestep him again and feint an attack, but he sees it and stops me in my tracks where I actually meant to go. "Sharing Kari," I say, disengaging. It's the first time I've actually admitted it to someone other than my mate.

Kent's laughing. Practically doubled over laughing. "No shit, Sherlock."

"What?" I've heard that phrase before, though I don't exactly know the human context for it. When you live as long as the we do, the cultural references come and go.

"None of us would be shocked to hear that. It's clear that you do," he says.

I tighten my hand around the hilt of my weapon, lucky that's made of a material that won't snap or bend. "I am trying."

"We know that too, Aeric. It's okay to admit that this is difficult. It is."

He attacks first, and I defend. Have I been so obvious? I suppose I hadn't much hidden the fact that I wanted Kari, and that I wanted her alone. Every time our sex has been separate, with the exception of saving her life. Even with the others in the room, I touched her alone so that she was only mine. "I've seen the ways it can go wrong," I say. "And I don't want that for any of us. It would be miserable."

Kent stops and raises a hand, reaching behind and unlacing the vest he's wearing. The ones we were all wearing. "Fuck I don't know how you all do that." He tosses it aside. "That's better. And you know what I've learned? Trying to avoid something because of the past usually ends up helping you repeat it."

We exchange more blows, Kent throwing a furious strike towards my head. I duck to avoid it, and his blade glances off one of the trees. I never thought that I would enjoy sparring with a human, but Kent is talented in this arena. If he were fae, he would be formidable, and possibly able to take me on.

Though I would never tell him that.

"You have a suggestion?" I ask.

"Yes," he says. "In this case, go against your instincts."

We've fought our way through part of the garden, and there's a stone bench here on the outside of the labyrinth. Out of the corner of my eye I can see the cascading waves of flowers from Kari's tree. And all around us are the roses that poured out of her as well. Sitting down, I catch my breath. "That's not an easy thing."

"Of course it isn't. But you can remember me as an example if you need to."

I raise an eyebrow and give him a look. "Really?"

"I was ready to tear your head off when we met," he said. "Every instinct that I had—and many that I still do—tell me that fae are dangerous and that they can't be trusted. That I should attack on sight. If I'd done that, where would we be now?"

I put down my sword and stretch. "It's not quite the same though."

"How?" Kent counters. "It's something that is now a part of my life, and that I'll have to fight against forever. That's what this will be for you."

Fuck. I hate that he's right. "I would like for it to go away entirely."

"It might," he shrugs. "Hopefully we'll have a lot longer to figure that out. But it's not going to go away if you keep holding on to the worry that it won't."

I drop my face in my hands and sigh. That spiral of jealousy I felt when Kari announced that…it felt like it was going to consume me. I let it go as fast as I could, but it's lurking under the surface. A shade or specter ready to jump out at any second. "I can't believe I'm asking you this of all people," I say, and Kent smirks. "But what do I do?"

To his credit, he becomes serious again. If he hadn't I might have had to do more than spar with him. Kent is easier to talk to about this than the others, even though I've known them longer. They don't understand it the way that he does. To them, a mating bond was the pinnacle of their hopes and wants. Until Kari, it was always a nightmare to me.

"Lean into the discomfort," he says. "It's not necessarily fun advice, or the best, but it has worked for me. The more you experience something, the more normal it seems to you."

"I suppose it's worth a shot."

Kent sits down on the other end of the bench. "You love Kari, right?"

"You know that I do." The words are practically a snarl.

"Then do it for her. I know you already are, but when I put things aside for her, it gets easier."

It does. That's something I've already noticed. Fuck. Taking a deep breath, I do what he's suggesting and lean into the feeling. I confront the discomfort of knowing that she's mating with two other men. Creating that same intimacy that she and I share, with them. She's going to carry all of us in her heart. And that thought makes it a little better. "I thought when I was happy for her and Brae that it was better."

"It's not a straight line," Kent says. "It never is. And you know that she needs this."

"I do know that." I can feel her easing. Relaxing. Letting the pain fade away into something else entirely, and for that—even if it's temporary—I'm grateful. "Thank you, Kent."

He smirks again and stands. "Don't make a habit of it. Now fight me before she calls us up there."

"Don't think I'm going to hold back just because you gave me some advice."

Squaring his shoulders, he stands across from me, mimicking the way I spin my sword in my hand with ease. "Wouldn't dream of it."

CHAPTER SEVENTEEN

KARI

Shivering pleasure rolls across my skin, and I arch off the bed, orgasm taking me by storm. Urien's mouth is between my legs, and holy fuck the man has a talented tongue. I tried to fall to my knees and mate with both of them, but neither Urien nor Verys would allow that. Instead they undressed me slowly, tasting my skin and arousing me with magic until I was a shaking mess pinned between them.

Being with them together is being like night and day. Verys is so pale and white in contrast with Urien's skin that's like the navy summer night sky. I want them. I want to know how they taste and how that magic will truly feel once it's kindled between my ribs. And still, Urien isn't stopping. He licks into me with abandon, and every stroke of his tongue is a show of fireworks and a cascade of sparks.

Verys has been touching me in other ways. Teasing my nipples with lips and teeth and drawing lines with his fingers for his magic to follow. I need both of them. Right the fuck now.

"Come here," I tell Urien, and he does. I pull him up my body, guiding him where I want him to be. Straddling me so his cock is within reach. It's beautiful—just as dark as the rest of him with paler lines of blue swirling across the tip. He groans when I touch him with my fingers, low and feral.

I like the way that sounds, and the way heat pools low in my belly in response. Starting slowly I only taste him with the very tip of my tongue. Using those blue lines as a guide, I trace along them and watch as his cock jerks and abs tighten. Those golden eyes stare down at me with molten fire, and all I can do is grin up at him.

I start to taste the bits of magic as I lick his skin, seeing images of a dark clear sky and winter bonfires. Feel the wind in my hair and smell snow. I lick the head of his cock, trying to savor every bit of him. He pushes into my mouth, and I don't stop him. I want more of him. This is not the same kind of control as Aeric. This is opportunity and need. Urien feeds himself to me until I can take no more in this position, and he curses as he pulls back and feels the friction of my lips on his skin.

Verys's hands are on my legs. Magic rising to the surface to meet his fingers. He enters me in one long, smooth stroke and I cry out around Urien's cock. Oh, to be full of them is pure magic, and that same magic is reaching for them. *Yearning* for them because it knows what's coming.

I'm distracted by the way Verys is plunging into me, the length of him reaching so deep that I already see those same stars from Urien's magic. It's his hands on my face that draw me back to him. He frames my face with his hands, pumping his hips into my mouth faster. As our power begins that tangling together, it's like taking that first breath of icy air walking into the cold. Like nothing has ever felt more clear and distinct.

One moment their movements are opposite, one cock impaling me and then the other one. Pleasure rings out through my body in waves, and I go over the edge into bliss again. Urien tastes too good to me, I wrap my arms around his hips and take him deeper. Sucking him in long slow pulls that match the swells of my climax. *Fuck* yes.

Then they're no longer opposite, but their movements are lined up together. Perfectly in sync to drive into me at one time. Now I can't do anything but feel. Surrendering to them, and the coming sensations. Urien's dark power twines with mine like rope, twisting together in a tight coil, ready to fuse together.

He takes his cock in his hand, stroking the portion that's not trapped between his lips. "Open your mouth," he says, voice rough. "I want to see you taste it."

I do. The tip of his cock rests on my lower lip, and Urien closes his eyes, working himself with his fingers. It's only seconds until he spills himself across my tongue, sweet magic splashing as his eyes fly open. It's a mouthful of power and I swallow it, savoring the taste of night and stars, and that thread connecting us merges, power passing into one and then the other. I feel him settle in my heart, and the way he's looking at me…

I can feel his raw gratitude and awe that we were chosen to be together like this. He looks at me like I'm the only star he sees and will ever see. Forever. *Yes.*

Pleasure spikes in my gut, Verys still taking his sweet, slow time fucking me. Urien has other plans. He rolls off me and moves, before moving me. I'm almost dizzy with it, now on all fours in front of Verys, and Urien thrusting deep into my pussy from behind. "Take him," he says. "While I take you."

I don't need to be told twice. Verys's cock is long and icy white. I've had it in my mouth before—when he stopped me from finishing the job, and I'm nearly salivating over him now. His skin is wet from being buried in me—I can taste myself on his skin. Every time Urien drives into me I'm fucked further onto Verys's cock, and there's something so fucking hot about it that I nearly come again from that feeling alone.

Verys weaves long fingers into my hair, guiding me so I am forced onto his cock in just the right way to make him groan. Silvery power seeps into my skin, and my own magic rises to meet it. This time it feels like a sphere. Like his power is cradling mine in a bubble and we're melding and expanding into one mass for each other.

"Goddess, Kari," he breathes. "I'm close."

The words make Urien move faster. Fuck harder. His hands are on my hips, yanking me hard back onto his cock. He runs traces of magic down my spine and drags them around to my clit, not letting me breathe even for a second. Now that he can feel my pleasure, he's using it to his advantage. I'm spiraling down into that sea of perfect bliss. Can't breathe, can't see, fingers gripping the sheets just to hold on.

Verys hardens even further in my mouth, and he goes stiff, suddenly holding himself deep. Silver white and shimmer explode through my mind. He tastes like a dream and a cloud and the mist of early morning. The way our magic blends is easy and natural—like it should have been that way all along.

Four sparks now rest in my chest. As distinct as light and darkness.

Urien pounds into me, holding me close as he comes again. His pleasure feeds mine. The power from this, I can feel it sinking into my bones. Exactly what we need for what we have to do. But we'll need more. Absolutely everything.

I can feel the emotion brewing in Verys when I kiss him. That sweetness is something I'll always cherish. Something I definitely want to explore with him when we have the time and space. "Get the others," I whisper. "We can't let the magic fade."

Verys kisses me hard for a moment, and that kiss tells me everything that I need to know about how he feels. The depth of his love and need for the bond that we've just created with each other. Then he's gone out of the room, and Urien releases me.

I try to catch my breath, but I'm not sure that's possible. Not with this much magic and emotion. Urien lays down beside me, pulling me to him and letting me rest for a moment on his chest. "This is the way I always hoped that it would feel," he says. The words *I love you* ring so clearly through our bond that I swear that I can almost hear them. I pull him closer. It's perfect.

Footsteps sound, and I don't move until hands find my waist. Brae guiding me away from Urien and Aeric is here too. Kent stands away. I want him in this. He is a part of this. But he knows that he won't contribute to the power that we're raising and is willing to sacrifice for it.

We're mated. Every one of us that can be, and in the same space it feels overwhelming and beautiful and I want to weep. Is one person really supposed to be able to hold this amount of love at once?

Aeric pulls me on top of him on the bed. He's already naked. When did he take off his clothes? Everything is pleasure and fire and magic and that's all I can see or feel. When he enters me, I close my eyes, falling into that gorgeous surrender with him. And he doesn't hold back, fucking me hard. Thrusting upwards deep into me.

Brae palms run down my back, spreading warmth and light over my skin, pressing me down into Aeric's chest. Aeric is here. Participating with the others. Tears well in my eyes from the joy. He's here with me.

"I'm here with you," he whispers in my ear. "And Brae and I are going to fuck you together."

I go still. We've never done that before, even though I've wondered what it would feel like. Two of them at once? I might die from how good it is. Fingers with cool liquid touch my ass, and I gasp. This is happening now. Oh, *Goddess*. I nearly come, squeezing down on Aeric's cock and feeling myself grow so wet that he slides in farther.

"Breathe," Aeric commands in my ear. "Relax and take him."

Brae presses a kiss to my spine before fitting himself against me. My heart is hammering in my chest, but I try to obey and keep breathing. Verys strokes a hand down one of my arms, and Urien the other, filling me with power and absolutely overwhelming me with magic. That's when Brae moves his hips, pushing past that barrier with silent ease, and I cry out. I've never been so full. Never in my life. And only the tip of him is inside me.

The way Brae feels right now is indescribable, both in reality through our connection. His pleasure is so sharp it makes me gasp for breath, and he wants more. He wants to move and take me all at once. It's taking everything for him to hold back. Sinking into me, he pushes slowly, and I'm blind with it. Aeric whispers encouragement and confidence in my ear. I'm being split open in the best way. Can barely catch my breath.

I feel Brae behind me, hips pressing against my ass. Goddess, he's all the way in me. And so is Aeric. Everything in my body is so sensitive, someone could blow on my nipples and I might come. But they're holding still. They're giving me a chance to adjust, but I'm not sure that I'll ever adjust to having two cocks in me.

And then they start to move, and I know I'll never adjust. I'll also never get enough.

Magic rips through me, light exploding through the room. It slams into all of us, power shining under my skin. One thrust and I come, and they're still going. Power sings in my mind, and I let it flow through me and out to them. They can use it. Shape it. It's exactly what we need.

Moving as one, Aeric and Brae drive into me. I can feel both of them moving with and against each other, every movement a new symphony of pleasure that I'm unable to name. I think I may scream, or have screamed. One never-ending orgasm. Outbreaks that fade to curlicues and rise into crests and ripples. The influx never ends.

There's nothing else to do but what Aeric told me to. Breathe. Relax. Enjoy. Pleasure has its way with me. Drenching my mind and body. I feel it when they come together, deep heat spreading and throwing out one last blast of power before we sink together. I am once again a vessel for magic. But this time it was all mine.

Arms cradle me as I sink into sleep.

CHAPTER EIGHTEEN

KARI

I'm lying in a bed, but it's not my bed. The light here looks strange and slightly hazy. I've never been in this room before, but the walls seem familiar. Pale and shining. Maybe moving? What is this place?

"Kari?"

I turn my head, and I'm lying next to Kiaran. *Oh.* This is *his* bed. And even though there's a blanket over his waist, he's not wearing any clothing. My eyes wander up his body, perfectly dark golden skin and the shapes of his abs that make my mouth water. He's long and lean and perfect. A swimmer's body, and I would happily swim with him.

I'm naked too, because I'm naked in bed at home. "Hi."

He's been looking at me too, and when he reaches for me I can feel him. But I know that he's not real. This is not what it will be like face to face. He pulls me close quickly, kissing me, allowing his hand to roam across my hip. "You're here."

"It's a dream."

He growls. "You think I care?"

There's a bandage over his shoulder, and I trace it. "You're hurt."

"It was nothing," he says quickly, "that was a good move on his part. I wish I hadn't stood in the way."

I close my eyes. "Does it hurt?"

Kiaran shakes his head. "No more than being here. No more than her having me. No more than what really touching you feels like."

"You're the only one," I say, tracing his lips with my fingers. "The only one that I haven't mated yet."

He rolls over me, and arousal blooms low in my stomach. The urgency in his kiss takes his breath away. "I don't care," he says. "I just want to feel you."

The shrill voice shoves ice into my veins and down my throat. "So this is what you do when I loosen my control." Ariana is standing in the doorway to this room. That smile that makes my skin crawl appears, and Kiaran throws himself off me. "Oh, dear," she says. "It's far too late for that."

"Get out," he says to her.

"Now now, where are your manners?"

The fury in his gaze could burn the world down. "Get *the fuck* out."

"Last time I checked, you were bound to me,

Kiaran," she says smoothly. "That means I can do what I like with you. Even be in your dreams. And what a good one to witness. I'm glad I was bored this evening or I never would have known how lucky I am." Her gaze turns to me. "Coincidence that your mate is mine? Or are you just that unlucky?"

Horror closes my throat. She knows. I was hoping that she would never find out. Not until I had figured out a way to save him. Now she's grinning like she was gifted a puppy. I'm not saying anything. Nothing that could possibly give her any more ammunition.

"Seems like I have the upper hand, and you are out of time. You know where I am. Clever, finding me here and breaking that ward. Even if the alarms you set off still give me a fucking headache." She lifts a finger, and Kiaran rises from the bed. "What am I going to do with you?"

The finger that's controlling him taps against her lips. "Apologize."

Kiaran's entire body goes stiff. He's fighting her power and I can see it on his face. Orange and red and purple light swirl around her hand, and the words come from his mouth. "I'm sorry, Ariana." The inflection is flat and dead. Forced words and nothing more. I can still see him inside. He's not gone yet, and if her magic wasn't holding him back he'd tear her apart. She knows that too.

A smile. "On your knees."

Suddenly the magic clicks in and his face melts into calmness. He bows his head and smoothly kneels before her. "I apologize, my lady. Forgive me."

She runs her fingers down his cheek and smiles almost fondly. My stomach turns. I want to break her wrist for daring to touch him. But even if I broke her here, it's still just a dream.

Ariana looks at me, gaze now frigid. "You are out of time. Be here by mid day. Alone. Or the next thing I will deliver to your home is the hearts and heads of both your friend and your mate."

With a flick of her wrist I'm falling, and I land in my own body with a jerk, snapping into a sitting position. I'm surrounded by sleeping bodies, none of us bothering to move after last night. It's already full bright. I'm not sure what time it is. "Wake up," I say. "We have to go. Now."

They're up and alert before I manage to make it all the way to the closet. "Slow down," Kent says. "What happened?"

"I can't slow down. There's no time. The deadline is now mid day, and she wants me to come alone. I know that you won't let that happen, so you need to be prepared for a fight. But unless we get there they're both dead."

"Who else?" Brae looks at me in horror.

"Kiaran," I say, pulling on the protective clothes that Kaya gave me for training and fighting. "She knows."

"Shit." Aeric flies off the bed. "Grab your weapons and clothes. Be downstairs in five minutes."

Faces are grim as they spring into action, but no one questions the validity of what I told them or argue a different path. I finish pulling on the pants and shirt. They're comfortable, and though I have little hope that the embedded protections would survive a direct blast from Ariana's power, it's a small comfort just the same. I use the last couple of minutes to braid my hair away from my face, all the while praying to the Goddess that we are not too late and we can manage to save them.

We wanted a plan, and we don't have one. But we have a lot more magic than we had before, and I can feel all four of my mates. Every one of them is focused and determined and confident. They're going to fight like hell for me. No matter what happens, I have that.

The portal is already open when I come down the stairs. They're all dressed and armed to the teeth with blades. Even Kent has a sword strapped to his back along with knives and the ash gun.

This is where someone might give a rousing speech in a movie. Rally up the troops. But this isn't a movie. There's no guarantee of a happy ending and no extra time. Instead, I push love through my bonds to them and take Kent's hand. We walk through the portal together.

CHAPTER NINETEEN

KARI

Everything feels different when we enter the tunnel again. The melted walls are still there, and the traps, but everything is silent. Not in the way it was—fake and hiding something sinister under the surface. No, everything is just...off. The traps are dormant, and there's a line of magic leading a clear path straight to her.

I guess Ariana is confident enough in my loyalty to both Kiaran and Emma that she's willing to risk me walking straight in. "Stay on your guard," Verys says. "She's not stupid enough to think that you'd actually come alone."

"No," I say. "She's not."

As we walk lower into the tunnels, it grows dark. There's no natural light, and we have to supply it with magic, but it also grows louder. After our third turn, rotating ever downwards, it becomes clear why this field of ice is in the Wild Kingdom. Because it's not a field of ice at all. The walls have melted into running water. Running, but static. It flows around the space of the tunnels like the air is solid.

Reaching out, I run my finger across the surface. It's so cold that I pull back, but I could plunge into it if I wanted. There's no barrier stopping the water, it simply *is*. Soon there's no ice left, only the flowing tunnels that lead us deeper down. The air is cold and thick with moisture. Colors from everyone's magic refract through the moving flow, lighting up the paths like a kaleidoscope.

I really don't want to think about how far we are under the surface. I can feel it. The pressure in my bones and the gut deep knowledge that the solid weight of the earth is above my head. Surely Ariana knows that I'm here by now? That I'm on my way? What time is it on the surface? Have we reached mid-day?

More twists and turns and with every one the anxiety builds in my gut. Knots upon knots of it, ready to make me scream. I have no idea how long we've been walking when the path levels out, leading us straight and away down a bigger part than before. Almost palatial in size, the waterfalls pouring down each side.

It would be incredibly beautiful if it didn't feel like a fucking death march.

Without warning, the tunnel opens up into space, and you can hear how loud it is. The sound of falling water echoes throughout this cavern, and our little lights are swallowed up without anything to bounce off.

But light comes from above. Suddenly. Brilliantly. A sphere of bright white, though I can already see that it's laced through with the colors of Ariana's stolen power that I saw just hours ago. "I told you that you were predictable," she says, calling out from across the room. There's a ledge of ice at the back of the space, and she's fashioned a chair like a throne on it, lounging. Kiaran is by her side. He's completely encased in magic, so there's no question about where his current loyalty lies.

She continues. "I told you to come alone or I would kill them."

Other taken fae are scattered around the space. It reminds me of what Kiaran showed me at the Heart of Allwyn. And the ones that we saw yesterday. They stand between us and Ariana, dead faced and ready to do her bidding. There's a lot of them, but not so many I don't think we could win.

The traps down here are complicated. I'm not exactly sure what they do, but I feel the magical connections that are powering them. Not so dormant as the ones that we passed—just waiting. Ready to be triggered.

"I suppose I should thank you," Ariana says, standing. "You've made it easier on me. Now I won't have to track down each of your lovers and kill them. I can do it all in one go."

"Where is she?" It's the first thing that I've spoken, and I'm taken aback by the way my voice sounds. Far, far more confident than I actually feel inside.

Ariana smiles, and gestures to the falling walls of water. I never would have noticed, but there's a shape inside the water. A bubble. Emma hangs suspended inside. Her form is to obscured by the rushing flow for me to tell if she's alive or even conscious. That water nearly took my finger off with its temperature. Getting to her isn't exactly going to be easy, and there's a crowd of fae that I have to get through first.

A cube of water containing Emma's bubble emerges from the wall, sliding across the slippery floor. It slides to a stop. "She's right here. Perfectly preserved, as promised. Though you broke the rules, and I'm not sure why I shouldn't just kill her now." Emma drops like a rag doll in the bubble, crumpling on the bottom of it from where she was floating. Emma looks frozen. If Ariana dropping her suddenly opens her up to that temperature, she doesn't have much time. Through the water I see Emma lift her head. She's alive. For now. I push down the fear that's squeezing my heart like a vise. I can do this. There has to be a way.

Reaching inside, I push confidence through the bond to my mates. They're not going to like what I'm about to do, but it's the only thing that I can possibly think of that might work. "I want to make a deal with you."

She tilts her head. "Whatever for? I have all the leverage."

"No," I say. "What you have is a stalemate. You have my best friend and my mate. You can't kill them and ever hope to get anything from me voluntarily. Ever. And you won't let them go because you need that leverage."

I feel the range of emotions from the men around me. From shock and panic to curiosity and trust. But there's only one person that I can't feel, and he's the one that makes the move. I hear the click of a hammer and look over to see Kent leveling the gun at Ariana. I think my heart stops for a moment.

As one, the fae look at us. Before they were looking straight ahead, and now their malevolent focus is chilling. Ariana doesn't flinch in the face of the gun. But she raises her hand to either side of her. Emma is lifted off the floor of her cage, and Kiaran stiffens beside her. "I could snap both their necks before that bullet hits me and we both know it."

"Kent," I say quietly. "What are you doing?"

"Giving her something to prove," he whispers back.

Ariana snaps her fingers. and around us within the water and under the surface of the floor I feel magic swim to life. The traps are primed, and if we walk forward at all we'll be caught in them. So will the fae that she has bound to her if she ever lets them move.

She stands up from her chair and comes down the steps, lazily walking through the rows of fae until she's close enough that I can see her face clearly. Kiaran follows her, eyes boring straight ahead like he sees nothing. But he's still held in her grip and so is Emma. "Have your dear mates ever told you what happens when fae die?" Ariana asks.

Her tone is so confident that I pause, and don't say anything.

"All power is a gift *temporarily* from the great and mighty Goddess. And Allwyn, of course. And when fae die, that power returns to the source. Or, if you're clever enough, it gets diverted to another one. A better one. So there's a flaw in your plan, Kari. I don't need you alive.

"Would this work better if you were? Yes. The power you have is far more potent within you. But I'll make do. And when your mates are dead as well, all that magic will be mine, and I'll have more than enough for what I need." She waves a hand, and the water closes over the entrance behind us.

Kent still has the gun pointed directly at her heart. "And if you die?" he asks. "What happens to the magic that you've stolen?"

"Your magic will be collected here after you are dead. Everything is ready. I misspoke before. I don't hold all the leverage. I hold all the power. And when you have that, there's no need to make deals. Especially when you know exactly what your opponent will do. You can create a situation she is unable to walk away from, and have her exactly where you want her." She's close enough now that I could reach out and touch her, but I'm terrified of what will happen if I do. "Goodbye, Kari. I'll make sure your magic is well taken care of."

There's a swell of magic and portals start to open. One near Emma's cage, and the other behind Ariana. A manic little smile crosses her face, and she reaches her hand for Kiaran's who takes it. She's planned this to the letter. Every possibility thought of, because she thinks she knows who I am and what I'll risk. So she doesn't see it coming when I grab the gun from Kent's hand and fire.

CHAPTER TWENTY

KARI

*E*verything happens at once.

The bullet flies towards Ariana, aim true. Time slows down, and I can feel the beat of my heart with every breath. She catches the bullet, magic wrapped around her hand and stopping it from piercing her heart, but she screams all the same. A horrifying scream of pain and rage that shakes the cavern and releases the fae on us.

I don't have time to think. I reach for Emma's cage and shove it as hard as I can with my power, causing it to skid away from the portal it was about to sink into. It crashes into the ledge of ice, cracking it. In the time that takes, Kiaran and Ariana are gone, the magic from their portal evaporating into thin air.

And around me, my men are fighting. The fae are not holding back. Ariana has given them instructions to kill. They don't have a choice. Their gazes are lit with bloodlust and fury that will only be sated by our death. One slides under Verys's blade and comes straight at me. Dropping the gun, I hold him back with my shield just long enough for Aeric to slam the hilt of his sword into his head.

The fae crumples in front of me, and all I can see is the peaceful innocence on their unconscious face.

"Kari, move," Aeric bellows.

Emma. I need to get to Emma. Aeric clears a path for me, and I sprint across the space to the cage. I feel the traps trigger, and I hit the floor just fast enough to avoid that spew of flame that almost killed me yesterday. I crawl underneath it through the melting floor, and scramble away from a pit that yawns open to my right.

The cube is right in front of me, and she isn't moving inside of it. "Emma!" I scream her name as loud as I can but there's no response. Her lips are blue and her skin is growing paler. She's going to die if I don't get inside there. I stroke the cage with magic. There's an opening at the top, but it's a one-way door. Once I go in, there's no coming out.

Fuck that. I'll blast my way out if I need to, but I'm not going to sit here and watch her die. Aeric appears at my side, breathing hard. "What do you need?"

"Keep them back long enough for me to break her out." Already fae are swarming towards us, not diverted by the other battles ranging around the room.

He nods, and sends a blast of green power into the fae running directly at him. The body goes flying into the opposite waterfall, and I don't see it again. I will mourn for these innocent fae later. I can see everyone trying to hold back their fatal blows, but it's just not entirely possible.

A shout draws my eye, and my stomach drops. Kent sprung a trap. Boulders of ice springing from the ground around him, encasing him, and slowly enclosing. He'll be crushed in less than a minute. *No*. The horror I feel is not just my own. I see it on Aeric's face, and feel it through our bond. Horror and outright terror for his friend.

"Save him," I say. "Please."

I'm climbing up the ice and clamoring over Ariana's broken throne as I say it. Emma could have less than a minute. "Aeric. Save him and then save me."

He hesitates for only a second, and I feel it. I'm his mate. He's sworn to protect me at all costs, and everything in him doesn't want to leave my side. Especially now. And then I feel him shift. This is his family, and every member is equally important. Even Kent. I feel him embrace this as something he wants and needs instead of fighting against, and then I see him *launch* across the space towards Kent.

That's all I see. I drop into the cage, through

freezing water. So cold I think it might kill me, and even after I drop inside the bubble there's no change. I'm shaking with it, but I pull Emma into my lap. She's cold and stiff, but alive. Barely. Her breath is shallow and the pulse I feel may as well be nothing.

I draw up as much power as I can, willing heat into the air around me and into her body. Enough so that I can get us out of here. I push against the opening at the top, but that's no use. It's sealed with enough magic to make it impossible.

Outside the cage, I hear my name, but I can't see anything through the movement of that water. But things are suddenly clear as the water slows, and stops. The magic laid on the entrance above me starts to shift, and I go cold with brand new terror. The cube is solid now. Red light flows across the outer edges of this box, drawing glyphs in jagged marks that I've never seen before, but are like the one that rendered Ariana invisible. I know by the dark energy coming off them that this is old magic. Older than I've been alive and likely older than my mates.

It fuses with the cube and locks it. One solid piece now. Unbreakable. And no holes. No air. The bubble Emma and I are in is small, and I haven't been conserving any oxygen at all. Already the walls are drawing condensation, and I notice that the air feels thin.

She even planned for this. Knew that I would try to save Emma at any cost, and thought of a way to get what she wanted. Placing my hands directly on the surface of our cage, I reach down and do what I never wanted to do again. I plunge into the well of the Goddess's magic entirely, and unleash it.

It melts the surface of this ice or diamond—whatever the hell she's trapped me inside of—but nothing more. The magic she's chosen isn't magic, I realize. It's a binding. Old enough to have been used against the gods. Ariana is hell-bent on killing Cerys. I don't know how deep or how far she searched for a way to trap this kind of power, but I feel it. I know that it's older than the remaking itself, and if I used every ounce of power I was given, it will not be enough.

Outside, I see my mates running. They realize what's happening and are blasting the outside of the cube with magic and their blades, trying anything to get through. But that won't work. I know it won't. Brae flinches away from the cube when he rests his hand on it, flesh burning.

I'm calmer than I probably should be. But this is why I wanted to make sure I mated with them. We knew that this might happen, and Ariana forced our hand. I push all the love in the world at them through our bond. Everything is hazy, and there doesn't seem to be enough air. Why is that? I pull in another breath and another, but it's thin like I'm on a high mountain. I can't remember why.

I lay down beside Emma. It was so nice of her to visit. The thought floats through my head like mist burning off in the sun. I wish she would do it more often. The last thing I hear is gunshots.

CHAPTER TWENTY-ONE

KARI

*D*eja vu. That's what I feel right now. Am I really awake? Didn't this happen just recently? Where I was pinned between Verys and Urien, pretending to be asleep? But that morning I don't remember everything hurting like this. Why does everything hurt? Again? I thought that I wasn't cursed anymore.

"Ow," I say. "What happened?"

Verys's eyes fly open, and I feel the overwhelming joy he feels, followed by him trying to be gentle with me even though every instinct in him wants to crush me to his chest. I take a deep breath, and my lungs ache. Suddenly everything comes flooding back, and I sit up in spite of the pain. "Emma. Where is she?"

I nearly leap off the bed, and Urien catches me around the waist and hauls me back. "Hold on, Kari. Take it slow."

"I need to see her."

Verys takes my hands and holds them. "Okay. But you need to rest as well." But he releases me. "She's down the hall."

I hate the fact that I feel weak, and I ignore the fact that I'm in pain, going straight for the door that I don't recognize on this floor. Emma is lying in a beautiful plush bed, the bright turquoise bedding is so her, that I have no doubt the house made this room to allow her to be the most comfortable. Her eyes are open, and she's staring at the wall.

"Emma," I say, rushing to the bed, but she doesn't really respond. After a minute she seems to notice that I'm there, eyes drifting over to meet mine. The emptiness in them is terrifying. She's not taken the way Kiaran is, but that doesn't mean that there wasn't a cost to this. "How are you?"

"I don't know," she says softly.

After a long silence, I lean over and hug her. "You're safe now."

She slowly shakes her head. "I don't remember most of it. There were…dreams. Terrifying dreams. And when there weren't, there were—" she cuts off. "It's all fuzzy."

"Everything will be fine," I tell her. "You're safe now."

Looking over my shoulder, I see Urien hovering. I didn't even think to ask, but I need to. "I'll be right back."

"Is she okay?" I ask him, stepping into the hallway.

Urien crosses his arms and sighs. "Physically, yes. I was able to repair all the damage done to both her and you. Mentally, I think only time will tell."

"Okay, thanks."

He puts a hand on my arm. "I have guards ready for when she wants to go home. She won't be unattended."

"Thank you," I say, smiling, "but I want her to stay here for now."

"Of course." He kisses my forehead before departing.

I need to go talk to my other mates so they feel that I'm alive. But I also need to make sure that she's all right. "Listen," I say, sitting back down on the bed. "You can stay with us for as long as you need to."

"No." The word is loud and forceful. She's suddenly animated. "No, I don't want to stay here."

"I swear to you that it's safe," I say. "I promise. Nothing can get through the shield here."

Emma rolls to the other side of the bed and stands up. She already has clothes on. "I waited because I wanted to make sure that you were okay, but I can't be here. The shield doesn't matter to me. I can't be in Allwyn. I can't. *I can't.*"

Those last words are nearly a sob, and I freeze. Guilt builds in my chest. This, no matter what anyone says, is my fault. She's the one who has to live with it, but I do to. "Okay," I say. "That's fine. We can take you home."

"I'm sorry," she says without looking at me, and she hugs me quickly in the same way. "I just need to be home."

Emma disappears out of the room, and I'm left staring after her. That's not exactly what I had expected or hoped. But neither was it fair of me to have expectations of her to begin with, after what she just went through.

Brae finds me still sitting on her bed a few minutes later. "She's gone. Aeric took her home."

"Okay," I say, fighting the sadness. "We can't tell her about Urien's guards. If she doesn't want to be in Allwyn, she won't want fae anywhere near her. But she can't be left defenseless."

He smiles. "They'll be perfectly invisible."

Leaning into his chest, I let myself lean into the feelings of loss and confusion. "Is she going to be okay?"

"I don't know."

"Yeah." I reach for his hand and stop when I encounter a bandage. "You burned it."

Brae lifts me into his arms. "I did. It's healing well though." He carries me back to my bedroom, and lays me out on the bed.

I want to argue that I don't need to be in bed

anymore, but my body would really fucking argue that point, and now that they can feel me there's no way that I could even lie about it. "I don't remember much after that."

"The gun. It broke the sigils just enough that we could blast our way through the rest of it."

"Why would it do that?"

"Cerys. She knew that humans would need some sort of protection against gods and fae. It's more powerful than we let on. That gun saved your life."

"And Emma's."

I don't say anything more. Luck or fate? I'm again at those crossroads. I was told by the Goddess that Kent was meant to be here with me. And he was a New York City police officer—one of the only people with access to the weapon that could save me. All the luck and coincidences are getting harder to ignore. And that means that I have to trust fate. That I'm meant to have this power and to do something with it.

"Do you think I'm predictable?" I ask.

Brae laughs. "You're anything but. However, you're a good person, and I think that's what Ariana meant. You have loyalty to your friends and you care about people. That doesn't make you predictable, it makes you strong."

That's true. But if I can't ignore the coincidences

that line up around me, I can't ignore the fact that even with careful planning, Ariana has been steps ahead. She's reached out into the future to imagine every possible consequence, and prepared for all of them. That's how deeply she believes in what she's doing. And yes, in a way that does give her some of the power. I need to surprise her. Do something she doesn't believe I'll ever choose.

Aeric steps into the room, followed by everybody else. Outside, the light in the sky is fading. Brae kisses my cheek. "We had an idea, if you're all right with it."

Tingling anticipation tickles my spine, and I blush, because I have an inkling about what their idea might involve. "Oh?"

"For tonight, at least," he says. "We want to sleep with you. Here in your bed."

"All of you?" Given the size of this bed there's plenty of room, but we've only ever done that by accident before.

Aeric nods his confirmation. "All of us."

I laugh, aching happiness filling my chest. "I'm not going to say no to that. But you're all wearing too many clothes."

"I could argue the same thing," Verys says while he makes quick work of my pants. Brae tackles my shirt, and it's a mess of hands and limbs stroking my skin. Fleeting brushes of magic and teasing pinches here and there.

"I'm no match for five of you," I say, more than a little breathless at their attention. "You're going to kill me."

Aeric smirks at me. "Little deaths only, remember? But I'm not sure you should be allowed to come. Not until we've all had our turn."

My eyes go wide with shock. "No."

His smirk only deepens as he leans close to my face. "What did you just say to me?"

"It won't be possible."

Kent laughs, pulling me closer down the bed. "Let's find out." He strokes himself a couple of times before fitting his cock into my pussy. Even without magic, Kent is an excellent lover, and he knows which buttons to push to get me close. It doesn't help when mouths meet my skin, tongues tasting each nipple and a daring one teasing my clit from one side. Aeric kneels above my head, slipping his cock deep down my throat, working me in long strokes that are the opposite of Kent's relentless, delicious, pounding.

It's the first time all five of them have done this together. Even the other night Kent stood aside. Now I have cocks sliding in me from each direction and magic swelling inside me, threatening to break.

They're not holding back either. I gasp for breath when Aeric pulls back, and I beg them. "If you don't want me to come then you can't do this," I say. "You can't go this hard this fast." And Kent is going fast. He's hitting that place deep within that brings me close right away, and I can barely breathe. I'm overloaded with sensation on every front. And then Kent slows down. Deliberately pulling back even though he's close. His hand falls to his cock, stroking himself as he moves to my side and wraps my fingers around his shaft. "Finish me."

"See? On the contrary," Aeric says, not bothering to hide his joy or amusement from me. "I think we can do that pretty easily."

They move, Verys sliding home into my pussy as Kent takes Aeric's place between my lips. "You're all traitors," I moan, holding back for a moment. "Conspirators."

Kent pushes deeper, and my words are silenced. It's good too, because I'm dizzy with silvery, fiery pleasure. My entire body is a mass of arousal. So much that I can't breathe. There's no way I'll be able to stop myself. Not with the way Verys is cascading his power into me, creating ripples and tide pools of that gorgeous shining sensation. But just as Kent groans and spills himself down my throat, Verys steps back. His magic fades and that toe-curling orgasm that was within reach evaporates. I shout around Kent's cock, and he laughs, pulling back and taking his new position at my breast.

"How long did it take you to come up with this plan?" I ask. "The torture Kari plan."

Verys doesn't press himself into my mouth at first, instead offering his balls between my lips. *Yes*. Everything. I want everything. Every part of them the want to give me.

Urien drives into me. "I'm pretty sure that this is the plan to give our mate one of the best orgasms of her life."

I can't respond, mouth now full of cock again, but they keep going. Urien drives me so close that I scream in perfect, exquisite agony when it's taken away. And Brae uses my pussy for a slow, thorough fuck that makes my legs shake and back arch. I taste every one of them and my skin is painted with their lips. "I blame you for this," I say to Aeric when he steps between my legs. I'm high on sensation. I might as well be dynamite with a lit fuse right now.

He rubs the head of his cock over my entrance, teasing me. Taunting me. Letting a tiny bit of shimmering spice and power leak from him into me. Verys seals his mouth over my clit, and I'm positively aching with need. But I've come this far, and I need to hear him say it. "I'll happily take the blame for this," he says, sliding in. "Just one more, Kari."

Hands—not Aeric's—pull my legs wide. As wide as they're able so that I'm open. On display for these men who love me. Brae grunts, spilling sunny gold on my tongue, and I feel myself slip in to a state of nothing but perfect rapture and euphoria. It's pure and white, and I am made of it.

Aeric places a hand on top of my stomach, pressing, holding me down so that I don't move while he takes what he needs. All of this was his idea. To show me the change in him. That he wants us together as a unit. There's nothing scary here, just mutual love, satisfaction, and—tonight not withstanding—all the orgasms I could ever want.

It's no accident that he's the last one to fuck me. He wants to be the one to say yes to me. I pull his bond up to the forefront, and I push gratitude through it. And love. And everything I'm feeling. I fling it straight at him and close my eyes, sinking into surrender. Tonight I'm not just yielding to Aeric. I'm yielding to all of them. To the Goddess. To fate.

Aeric falters in his rhythm, and in that bond I feel him grow so close. His eyes lock on mine, and he smiles, and nods. He doesn't tell me when, or command it, it just happens. One moment the pleasure is rolling through me, and the next minute it's consuming me. I'm a super nova ready to burn the world down with the magic that I've been given. I'm a girl so far in love with these men that I can't see straight. I'm caught in a storm of magic, but this kind doesn't want to eat me alive.

My scream is one only of molten bliss, and whatever pain I had is banished from my body. It feels like being at the core of a sun and perfectly content with the heat. I will happily be engulfed in these flames.

Every single one of them is touching me when I recover. My head is pillowed on Brae's chest, and Aeric has an arm slung around my hips. Hands and fingers tangled everywhere, and it feels as natural as breathing.

Urien chuckles softly. "Told you."

"I will admit that you're right," my voice is scratchy from the screaming and their use of my mouth. "But that's not something we can do all the time. You're going to give me a heart attack."

"Maybe we should rethink the term 'little death,'" Brae says absently, running his fingers through my hair. "That seemed like a pretty big death."

"Don't change it unless you want a fight with the French," Kent says, and I can almost hear him rolling his eyes.

Verys raises his head. "Is there a story there that we need to know about?"

"Don't ask," he mutters, and I collapse into laughter.

"I love you," I say, fighting through the giggles. "Every one of you."

Aeric's lips meet my ribs in a gentle kiss. "Even when we torture you?"

"Even then, I'm afraid."

We grow quiet then, and in the gathering darkness, some of them sleep. I don't. I'm actively burying my thoughts so they don't sense them. Nothing will ever make me happier than this—being loved and accepted by these men. But the danger isn't over. Not by a long shot. They would all walk into hell for me without question, but I don't want them to do that. I want them to be safe and happy and free.

The feeling in that hallway, when Emma was gone, I don't ever want to experience that again. And even though Emma is one of my best friends, losing one of these perfect, beautiful men sleeping with me would be a wound I'm not sure that I could ever come back from. I push that fear deep down low, where I'm sure that I'm the only one that will ever be able to find it.

Ariana thinks that I'm predictable, and she's

already thought of ways to hurt me. Torture me, kill me, and steal the Goddess's power while my body is still warm. So I need to take back that power.

Next to me, Aeric stirs in his sleep, and I brush the hair off his face. For once, I've exhausted them enough that they don't wake up at a simple change in my breath. My heart aches with love, and the knowledge of what's coming.

The only way I can see to beat Ariana is to take her by surprise. And to do that, my mates—my lovers—can't see it coming. They love me too much and too deeply to let me, and I love them too much to stop them. There's a chance in the world that it won't work. And that I'll die in the process. But it seems like I was chosen, and for the first time, it feels right to embrace that.

I cuddle closer to my mates and try to sleep, though my mind is racing. I know what I have to do.

To be continued...

Want to know what happens next? Aeric, Brae, Kent, Verys, Urien, and Kiaran are waiting for you *Breathless*.

KEEP IN TOUCH!

Devyn's Newsletter:

Be the first to hear updates about my new releases, sexy exclusive content, and the occasional dessert recipe!

https://www.subscribepage.com/devynsinclair

Devyn's Facebook Group:

Come hang out with us! We talk about books —*especially* the sexy ones—share memes and hot inspiration photos and more!

https://www.facebook.com/groups/devynsinclair/

ABOUT THE AUTHOR

Devyn Sinclair writes steamy Reverse Harem romances for your wildest fantasies. Every sexy story is packed with the right amount of steam, hot men, and delicious happy endings.

She lives in the wilds of Montana in a small red house with a crazy orange cat. When Devyn's not writing, she spends time outside in big sky country, continues her quest to find the best lemon pastry there is, drinks too much tea, and buys too many books. (Of course!)

To connect with Devyn:

ALSO BY DEVYN SINCLAIR

For a complete list of Devyn's books, content warnings, bonuses and extras, please visit her website.

https://www.devynsinclair.com/

Printed in Great Britain
by Amazon